Heart of Fire

M. KATHERINE CLARK

Other Works by M. Katherine Clark

The Greene and Shields Files:
    Blood is Thicker Than Water
    Once Upon a Midnight Dreary
    Old Sins Cast Long Shadows
    Tales from the Heart, Novelettes

Soundless Silence a Sherlock Holmes Novel

The Rest is Silence, an Edmond Holmes Novel – Coming Soon

Love Among the Shamrocks Collection:
    Under the Irish Sky
    Across the Irish Sea
    On the River Shannon
    The Land Across the Sea, an Emmet O'Quinn Short

Love Among the Shamrocks Collection,
    The Next Generation:
    In Dublin Fair City
    Song of Heart's Desire
    Chasing After Moonbeams – Coming Soon

The Wolf's Bane Saga:
    Wolf's Bane
    Lonely Moon
    Midnight Sky
    Star Crossed
    Moon Rise
    Moon Song, a Companion

Dragon Fire
    Heart of Fire
    Will of Fire – Coming Soon

Silent Whispers, a Scottish Ghost Story

*To the woman who inspired my strong heroines! My mother,
the strongest woman I know!*

Brigid

hey said I was a witch. Like my mother and grandmother. They called us evil, mistresses of Satan, their bane. They said we could talk to animals and we communed with the devil. But what they did nae ken, what they could *not* know was, witch was nae too far from the truth. Not that I practiced black magic or drank goat's blood from a skull, but I was a healer. The ancient Druidic practices of my people were well lost to time but there were worse things than to be considered a witch.

I kept to myself in the little cottage my mother left me. No one ever told me what happened to my parents, but I knew. My mother had been burned alive by the heathens who wanted to protect themselves. And my father fell in battle long before. I was but a child when my father kissed me on the forehead and told me to be good, before leaving the cottage. I remember seeing my mother crying as she held his tunic in her hands.

Then, she was gone too. Years of healing the clan and then ostracized by the church. I bear them no ill, for they believed anything they did nae understand was evil. But if I was, then why did the women of the clan come to me for remedies to prevent them conceiving, or when they needed help conceiving?

I stayed in my cottage and pretended the world around me was not falling apart.

Chapter One

Brigid

It was the thirteenth century and I was in Scotland. I rose with the sun, did my prayers, tended my garden, ate and slept at moon rise. That was what I always did, in all my twenty years.

As I stirred my porridge for my morning meal, a knock came at my door. I pulled my plaid *aristad* over my head and looked out to see who was knocking at such an early hour. Three men I had never seen before, knocked again.

"Mistress," one called. "We are the laird's guards. He has asked to speak with you."

The laird, the bane of my existence and my uncle. "What are your names?" I called out.

"This is Liam and Roger," he said. "And I am Kane."

"Kane?" I questioned.

"Aye, Brigid, 'tis I. We offer nae ill to you," he assured. "We have no weapons on our person apart from our wee knife."

"Send the others away, you know I am nae a threat to you," I called.

It was quiet for a moment until I heard Kane's voice speak again. "I have sent them away. Come out, Brigid."

Kane. He had been my best friend as a lass. One day he was fostered with a neighboring clan and I never saw him again. If it was in fact him, he had grown into a fine man. Opening the door, I gazed into the well-remembered brown eyes.

"Kane?" I breathed.

He smiled and I was taken back to my youth when the world was fair. I stepped forward and offered to embrace him. He wrapped his arms around me, and I took in his familiar smell. Peat, hide, and the musk of sweat, he must have trained earlier that day.

"'Tis good to see you, Brigid," he said pulling back. "I ken 'tis been a while."

"Years. What are you doing back?"

"Your uncle has called us all to return from our fostering," he replied. "He is troubled."

"By what?" I had not heard anything from the women who came to me for help.

"It would be better if he told you," Kane answered. "Come now, I brought my horse."

"It is not far to walk. I will be fine. I will be but a moment," I replied. Kane nodded slowly as I turned back to my cottage and doused the kitchen fire. "Lir, stay," I called to my deerhound who lounged beside the hearth. His lazy black eyes looked up at me and he huffed a sigh. Gathering my things, I took some herbs not knowing if I would need any and shut the door behind me.

"You have not changed," he said.

"I have grown," I answered.

"Well, aye into a fine lass, but I meant you are just as stubborn as I recall." He untied his horse from a tree and walked beside me.

"I cannae argue that," I agreed. "But tell me, why does my uncle wish to see me? It is not a usual request."

"As I said, he is troubled," he replied.

"By what?"

"There is a great threat at his door," he answered. "A threat none of us have dealt with before."

"And he believes *I* will know how to deal with it?"

"I ken no'," he dodged. "All I know is he charged us to bring you to him with all haste."

"And when I get there?" I asked, suddenly worried the same fate would befall me as it did my mother, the laird's own sister.

"I donnae ken," he answered.

"Kane," I pressed. "You know what they call me. You know what they did to my mother. Tell me truly, are you leading me to my fate?"

"Brigid, if I knew, I would tell you. But I was called to bring you to him that is all," he answered.

"Why you?"

"I suppose, he knew you may not trust another."

"I have nae reason to trust another, nor you, you have been gone for nearly ten years."

"We are here, Brigid please," he said. "Go to your uncle and see what he wants."

"And will you look me in the eyes as they lower the torch to my pyre?"

"They are not going to burn you," he stated harshly. "'Tis to do with…"

"Ah, so you ken what it is to do with," I cried. "Tell me!"

"Brigid," I heard my uncle's voice boom from the keep steps. Turning to him, I bowed and looked up at his grey eyes. It had been years since I had seen him, and the years had not been kind. His young, second wife stood, heavily pregnant, beside him, her eyes downcast. She was no older than me; sold by her family to the great laird of the isles one year ago. We had grown friendly over the last few months. I knew what she went through at my uncle's hand.

"Uncle," I said. "You have called for me. How can I help you?"

"I see you are as stubborn as my late sister."

My blood raged and my hands fisted. "Donnae dare speak of my mother! It was your hand that lit her pyre!" I spat.

"You will nae raise your voice to me," he bellowed. "I should have you whipped for your insolence."

"Then do it! You deserve my ire. You killed your own flesh and blood! You are a monster. And you are nae kin of mine! Let all here witness your atrocities. Let all here witness my curse."

"Enough! You have spent too long on your own, you forget I am your laird."

"So says the man who lead my father and his men to battle never to return," I answered. "Tell me now, did you call me here for a reason? Speak. And donnae forget my mother was older. If I were a man, I would be within my right to challenge you."

"Guards," he roared. "Seize her."

Screaming a battle cry my father taught me, I backed up away from the men who surrounded me, looking for the weakest. My father was War Chief and he taught me much on how to wound, maim and kill.

"Let any man who attacks me, beware. I will show no mercy."

My eyes locked with Kane. His bitter smirk told me everything.

"Tie her to the stake," my uncle ordered. "For once in her life, she may be useful to us."

The men grabbed me, but I fought them off, my fingers glancing off a sword. There were too many of them. Taught by their laird not to fight fairly.

"Donnae touch me! Give me a sword and fight me properly! I curse your family and your line for all eternity," perhaps they would stop, if they thought I was a witch. But their loyalty to their laird kept them grounded. Without a weapon, the guards soon overpowered me and tied me to a rough stake. My arms hurt and I was certain I had bruises from their biting grip. I stood helpless, praying for a miracle. I did not want to die. My eyes locked again on my so-called friend. Kane's face had changed to a young image of my uncle, hard, angry, and bitter. For the first time, I wondered who Kane's father was.

"Cur," I spat. "You were my friend."

"I am nae friend to a witch," he hissed.

"Aye for there can be only one serpent between us and 'tis nae I."

Kane stepped forward, an ugly sneer on his face, his hand on his sword.

"Silence," my uncle bellowed. "If she enjoys serpents and magic so much, she should enjoy one of her own. Leave her to him."

My eyes snapped to my uncle and grew wide. "To whom?" I demanded. Just as I spoke, a roar like I had never heard before, echoed in the bailey.

Chapter Two

Finn

I watched as the humans grabbed the lass. Her fighting spirit did her kind proud. From my vantage point, I watched and circled. It was not my desire to commune with the humans. Especially the Lewis. They were not to be trusted, but my father had declared it necessary and as his heir I obeyed. My three younger brothers were only too eager to pounce on me and my claim to the throne. They were too young by half and considered themselves invincible. Granted flying high and watching the humans with predatory eyes, clear as if I were on the ground, did give one a sense of being gods. But I knew better than most that we were not immortal.

When the human guards grabbed the lass, I was impressed by her fighting skills. Had she found a sword, I was sure more than one would bleed. But soon they overpowered her, and she was tied to a stake... for me. I wondered why she fought so. We MacKays were known far and wide for our lovemaking skills and we were fiercely loyal to our mates, forced on us or not. Why did she fight so? Then my stomach dropped when I heard her words. She did not know what was happening to her. She had not been given a choice. I could not help myself, I let out a loud roar. This was not what was agreed. I was to be given a *willing* lass, one who agreed to her fate, not one who was forced into it. Suddenly, all made sense and my estimation of her increased.

Her eyes rose sharply to the sky as I circled and landed with a mighty shake. A hush descended on the gathered humans. I was not sure if it was because of my sheer size that they were stunned into silence or if it was because of the lass. But whichever it was, they stared at my glistening green hide. My long neck whipped over to the laird. The old man motioned to the lass, trembling... I sniffed the air, not fear but anger.

"Take her, and may this be an end to it," the laird said. *An end?* I nearly shifted into my human form and charged him with his words. But my father had decreed no human blood was to be spilt. He did not, however say I could not scare him a little. Raising one of my talons, I covered one nostril and blew fire out of the other, just enough to startled those around me. The laird stepped back, "take her and go," his voice trembled.

Turning back to the lass, her hard blue eyes met mine and, by all that was holy, she was beautiful. Fiery red hair set in a pale freckled face and the bluest of blue eyes stared into my green ones. She was scared but refused to show it. As gently and softly as I could, I swiped at the ropes holding her. Seeing a fire behind her eyes, I whipped my tail around the stake, preventing her only route of escape. When she was free, she glanced around looking for a way to run, but eventually looked back at me and her eyes grew wide.

Had she never seen a dragon before? Did she not know the legends of the isle? Shaking my head, I gently scooped her up in my large talon, barely feeling her striking my scales. She wanted free, but she was mine and I would never let her go back to the humans who treated her as if she were chattel. I beat my wings, creating a massive gust of wind. The warriors covered their faces as the dirt beat about them. Finally, I jumped off my hind legs and into the air. The lass screamed as we left the ground, but I paid no heed and beat powerfully through the air and into the sky. The sooner we were on my clan's lands the better. My father needed to hear what happened.

Brigid

There is a dragon. I repeated but no matter how many times I said it, it did nae change the fact that a large green dragon dropped from the sky, clasped me in his talons, and flew away from my clan and the ground. Gripping tightly to the scales, I could not make sense of what was happening. Dragons were a thing of myth. We were living in the thirteenth century. There were no such things as dragons. Except... there was one, carrying me high above the ground. Scotland passed by below, all patchwork and dotted with cottages and keeps.

Keeping my wits about me, I located the sun beside us. South, we were heading south. South from the Islands of my ancestors.

"Ehm, dragon?" I called. The long snout turned down to look at me. The green dragon eyes, merely slits were questioning. "Where are we going?" It snorted. "I asked you a question, where are we going?" It said nothing only gripped me tighter. "I demand to know where we are going. Who are you?"

Finn

She demands? I chuckled to myself. The tiny human, whose weight I could barely feel, demands to know where we were going. *Oh, this will be fun.* When I decided to play with my human, I was nae sure. But as soon as I felt the pressure in the air drop, I free fell with it. She screeched and clutched my talon tighter.

"You did that on purpose!" she screamed. *Smart little thing,* I thought. My dragon grinned devilishly. Feeling the air was right, I folded my wings back and spiraled through the patch of wind. Flying backwards, I looked down as I clutched her to my chest. She was grasping to my scales but was not enjoying herself. Tears rimmed her eyes and it gave my dragon and I pause. She buried her face into the hard hide and wept. I felt the drops not only on my scales but in my heart as well. She did nae ken who I was, or what was going on. She had every right to ask, but I played instead of settling her fears. My dragon's protective side roared to life and I held her to me as I searched for a ledge to land. Eventually, I saw the waterfall on the edge of my father's land. It had a large cave behind it. Breaking through the water, I landed gently and shifted into my human form, still holding the lass to my chest.

Chapter Three

Brigid

I was crying like a bairn. Though it was an act, I could not stop. I thought I was to be killed, burned at the stake. But instead, I was stolen by a dragon and flown far away from my clan. Granted the clan never accepted me, but they were still my family. What about my animals? Who would look after them?

Slowly, I realized instead of hard scales beneath my cheek, there was now warm flesh. I looked up and saw a man with the greenest eyes I had ever seen, staring down at me. Shocked, I backed away from him and gasped when I noticed he was naked. The man looked down and seeming to notice, bent and untied a small pouch from his ankle.

Male form was not a foreign thing to me, as a healer I usually bathed men when they were too weak or sick with fever, but something about him felt wrong when there was no medicinal purpose to my perusal.

"'Tis all right, lass," his deep, velvety, baritone voice rumbled. "You can look now, and I apologize I was nae covered when you first looked. But I was more concerned with landing and shifting back."

"You... you were the dragon?" I questioned.

"Did you no' ken I was a shifter?" he asked.

"Know? How would I know anything about you?" I demanded. "You steal me away from my family, my clan and I am supposed to know who you are?"

"From what I saw, they were no family to you, lass," he answered. "They sold you to me without your knowledge."

My mother always warned me about my fiery temper and through the years I have had cause to regret it, but never so much as that moment. I flew at him, nails ready to claw those gorgeous green eyes out of his face. He gripped my wrists and held me off, but I kicked and screamed at him.

Finn

Fiery she-devil. She does her kind proud. I held her wrists as gently as I could, but she was stronger than I thought. My shins ached with her hard hits. I dropped one hand to hold her waist away but then felt a sharp sting, followed by hot liquid. Looking down, I saw the slashes on my chest and her wee eating knife stuck in my shoulder. I looked over at her, shock registering on my face. She had stabbed me! Her wee knife hidden in the folds of her stockings, was now in my shoulder.

She took my surprise to her advantage and kicked my knee out from under me. I heard and felt the crunch. A quick shout was all I had time for before I fell to one knee. At my lower height, she had the advantage. She grabbed the knife from my shoulder and tugged, the metal cutting me even deeper. She made a move to cut my throat. My dragon took over – always did when I was in danger – roared and shifted.

Towering over her, I looked down. She had fallen on her bum and stared up at me, tears back in her eyes. This time, I could scent fear. My shoulder and knee healed quickly with my advanced healing, but my pride was another matter. One thing I needed her to understand was, she was mine. Rearing back, I let out a roar and the burning acid in my throat expelled. The fire was hot, loud, and sudden but I made sure the lass was far from harm. It was a test to show her who I was, not a way to hurt her. I would never harm a lass, human or dragon. But my knee still ached from her attack though my opinion of her elevated.

Once the fire died and the noise had lessened, I heard it. She wept bitterly. She was scared. How I missed it the first time, I will never forgive myself. She had kept a façade of bitterness and strength, but now she wept. Looking away from her in shame, I hated what her family had done. It made me want to fly back there and, treaty be damned, burn their crops, village, and keep to the ground. My dragon urged me to avenge her. I did not understand why but for some reason I wanted to show the Lewis Laird he could not break the treaty and not expect retaliation. The MacKays were to be given one willing lass every twenty years. It was clear this one was not willing.

"Please," I heard her whisper. "Who are you? What will you do to me? Please donnae burn me alive."

That had my head whipping back to her. Burn her alive? This fighter, this queen in the making, the woman who took on six men back at the keep and who attacked me with nothing more than an eating knife, pulled her knees up and tucked them to her chest. She looked so young and in all my twenty-eight years, I had never felt a pull so deeply to any lass.

She did not look up at me, only looked around the cave, hoping for a way out. I shifted back putting my dragon's sense of hurt pride and need for revenge away. Wrapping my plaid around my waist, I secured it with my clan's brooch. When I took a step closer to her, she scurried as far back against the wall as she was physically able.

"I will nae burn you alive, lass," I confirmed. "I would

never hurt you."

"What do you want from me?" she demanded.

I bit my lower lip, how did I tell her, her clan had sold her to me without her knowledge?

"Can we start again?" I asked. "My name is Aodhfionn MacKay. I am the son of Edan, Chief MacKay of the Isle of Skye, King of the Dragon Shifters. I am his heir, a dragon shifter. Tell me your name, lass?"

"Brigid," she finally replied.

"Brigid," I smiled. "It is a pleasure to meet you. What is your position in Clan Lewis?"

She stared at me a moment, then, "I'm a witch," she answered.

Chapter Four

Brigid

It was wicked, but I could not stop the words. I had to use any method possible to make this dragonman let me go. My eyes were drawn to where I had stabbed him. The pink scar there caused my brow to furrow. It was healed already.

"A witch?" he asked drawing my attention back. "What do mean a witch?"

I took a deep breath. If I was to be killed, I needed to use everything in my power. "I mean," my strength returned. "A witch. And if you donnae let me go, I will curse your house for a thousand years."

For a moment, it looked like he believed me. But then, he threw his head back and laughed.

"Och, if this is nae exactly what we expected from Clan Lewis," he said. "A wench, not only unwilling, but a witch too?"

"I am not a wench," I stated. "And I demand you take me back to my cottage."

He sobered for a moment, then locked eyes with me. "You truly have no idea what is happening, do you, lass?"

"I know you abducted me. What more is there?" I questioned.

He huffed a sigh. "Let me get you to my clan and we will talk more then."

"No, I demand you take me back this instant."

He shook his head. "That is impossible I'm afraid, but there are some who may be able to help explain it better than I can. Come with me, lass."

I thought a moment. He had not hurt me, in fact I was the one who attacked him and even though he had every right to retaliate, he had not. The thought of going back to my clan turned my stomach. My uncle hated me and my one and only friend had betrayed me. But my cottage, my deerhound, my home needed me, and I had to find some way to get back even if he said it wasn't possible. Looking deeply into his green eyes, I slowly nodded.

"All right, MacKay," I said. "I will go with you for now. But please, no more of the fire."

"You are afraid of fire, lass?" he asked.

"No," I denounced. "I merely do not like having something so deadly near me."

"Verra well, I will not use fire unless absolutely necessary," he promised and extended his hand to help me up.

Slowly, in a sign of good faith, I took his hand and ignored the spark that flew between us. He helped me stand and motioned me to move as he walked a few steps toward the entrance.

I had never seen anything so fascinating. The sounds of crunching bone and tearing flesh was short. He did not even flinch when what sounded like every bone in his body broke. A snout elongated from his face, wings sprouted from his back, and scales covered his entire being. After mere moments, where once there was a man, now stood a dragon. His massive head turned to look at me. He offered his talon. Eyeing it, I looked up into the green slits.

"Could I not ride on your back like a horse?" I asked. He snorted and lowered his eyes to mine. "Is that not done?" He shook his massive head. "Well, I will nae ride in your hand." I crossed my arms over my chest. Finally, he snorted again and looked away for a time. Huffing a sigh, smoke curled out of his nostrils. I took a step back. He looked at me and again offered his talon.

Seeing my escape was blocked by his massive frame, I sighed and agreed. Before I could understand what was happening, he lifted me up to his neck and I slid down. Straddling, my legs rested on his shoulders. Unsure if it was a safer option as he beat his massive green wings and took off through the waterfall, I held on for dear life.

Finn

I tried to ignore the spark that had passed between us earlier when I offered her my hand. But with her legs gripping my neck, the soft feel of her calves pressed against my wings, and her breasts pushed against my neck, I was having difficulty concentrating where I was going.

We dragons were a physical lot and we enjoyed getting to know our females' bodies. But no matter what had passed between me and any dragon woman, the feel of this human clutching to me, trusting me, made me ache for more than just physical. She was everything I admired in a female. Strong, a warrior, skilled, fearless. Aye, she would make an exceptional queen. If I could not scent the human blood within her, I would have sworn she was dragonborn.

The sooner I could get her to the clan the better. Perhaps my mother or the women in our clan could help her understand what was happening. One thing was certain... she was mine.

Slowly, my father's lands came into view. The keep was carved into the mountain. The training field was to my right with our dragon clan flag fluttering in the wind on either side of the gate. It was an impressive sight and one that would soon be mine once my father stepped down. As usual, I prayed he would extend his reign and not step down in eight months as he planned. I was a warrior, not a king. But as his first born, it was my duty to take over for him, not something I looked forward to.

Circling the landing site, I slowly lowered to the ground. Once I was down, I raised my claw and offered it to Brigid. She wrapped her wee hand around my massive talon and I set her down on the sand. She stumbled for a moment, getting her legs back from the air as I shifted.

I could see my queen look around her. Taking in the land and people, or looking for a way to run, I was unsure. As soon as I had wrapped my plaid around me, I saddled up to her side. The crowd gathering near us, fell silent.

Whispering in her ear away from the dragons, I spoke low. "We have a long-standing history with humans. Please, at least pretend to be here of your own free will. I will speak with my father later and explain everything. Perhaps then, I will be able to take you back to your clan. If that is still your desire."

I could not help noticing the gooseflesh that rose her skin as my hot breath reached her ear. She responded to me well. She stared into my eyes and eventually nodded. I took her hand, again feeling the spark of dragon fire between us. Raising our hands into the air, I turned to my clan.

"Brigid of Clan Lewis!" I heralded. The dragons erupted in applause. "We go to my father. But we will be with you all at dinner. I ask you to pledge fealty to her then." The dragons shouted our moto and with a quick bow, they turned back to their work. Brigid and I were alone.

She turned to me. "I will have no one's fealty. I am not a chief."

"Nay, but as you will be part of our family," she did not know everything. I needed to tell her she would be their queen as soon as we were married and I was given the title from my father.

"Please," she began. "I want no fealty. I only want to go back to my cottage. I am needed. My… Lir is waiting for me."

My dragon roared inside my head. He wanted to know who Lir was.

"You are promised?" It wouldn't surprise me.

She looked around, clearly debating telling me the truth. I breathed easier. If she had to pause, then she was not with another male.

"No," she sighed. "I am not promised. I simply need to leave. Please."

I opened my mouth to speak but before I could say anything, Kai, my best friend and my father's War Chief approached. His usual randy smile lifting his lips.

"Finn, I have always been envious of you, but now?" His blue eyes skated over Brigid, making me growl. He chuckled. "Now now," he winked at me then looked back at Brigid. "Kai MacKay, my lady, a pleasure to meet you. Never thought this ol' man would find a lady of such grace and beauty."

She snapped her eyes to mine. I was sure she would understand soon. She was no sacrifice; we were to be married. But I hoped to speak with her first. Slowly, she looked at Kai and forced a smile. "I thank you for the compliment, Master MacKay," she said.

"Come let us go to my father," I said, gripping her a little tighter to me. Why, I had no idea, but I did not like how Kai was looking at her. He was two years younger than I but was also unmated.

"Ooh, donnae let the ol' dragon king bother you, my lady," Kai replied with a grin. "He's truly a pushover for a pretty face."

"I will ignore you calling my lord father... your king, old," I stated.

Kai laughed. "Nothing you have not said yourself."

"I am his son," I answered as if that justified my occasional playful tease to my father.

Kai merely grinned wider as I pulled Brigid across the landing ground and through the village to the keep. Once we were far enough away, I stopped for a moment.

"I am sorry," I said. "Kai is a randy lad, but he is my best friend."

"'Tis all right," she answered. "But why did he call me yours?"

"I must speak with my father first."

"Aodhfionn," she spoke my name and a shiver stole up my spine. It was the first time she had said it. We stared at each other for a long time before she spoke again. "I would rather hear it from you."

"'Tis a long tale, lass," my voice was low.

"If I am to be some sort of sacrifice to the dragons or you, I should know," she said. "'Tis my right to ken my fate."

She truly was afraid we would kill her. I wanted to know what trauma she had endured to make her suspicious of everyone.

I took her hands in mine, so small and looked into her eyes. "Aye, you are right," I replied. Looking around, I found the place to speak with her. "Come with me."

Taking her hand tighter in mine, I guided her toward the

cave cut into the wall of the mountain. We said nothing as I helped her climb. I realized too late it was not easy for her in her gown, but she was right by my side the whole way. Again, I admired her strength.

Finally, we reached the top and I gazed out. She grabbed my arm when her steps faltered. When she righted herself, I mourned the loss of her touch on my arm. She gazed out with me but soon she closed her eyes and rocked back and forth as if dizzy. I wrapped my arm around her and moved further into the cave.

"Are you well?" I asked.

"I—" she began. "Cannae be so high up," she confessed. "It makes my head light and I am dizzy."

I breathed a laugh. "So, let me see if I understand you correctly. You donnae like fire, heights, or flying," I replied. "And they gave you to us?"

Brigid crossed her arms over her chest and stared at me.

"I also donnae like men telling me what to do or teasing me for something I cannae control," she answered. "Now, if you brought me up here for any reason, it was to tell me why I am here. So, get on with it."

Chapter Five

Brigid

I had my fair share of people laughing at me, fearing me, hating me, and I could do nothing. Not so any longer. If he would ever explain the current situation to me, I would be better equipped to handle my escape. Aodhfionn sobered and looked at me for a few unnerving moments. His green eyes fixed on mine. I wanted to look away, but I refused to show weakness.

"Verra well, lass," he spoke low. "I will tell you why you are here." I watched as he sat on the ground beside me. With a sigh, he began. "Nearly three hundred years ago, dragons held all of the isles. We are mighty warriors and there were many of us. Soon the Saxon Invaders reached the islands and we fought. Many were killed. Among those who fell was the king and his eldest son. Once the second born son realized his father and brother were killed and he was king, he mourned and, in their name, drove the Saxons back. At the end of the day, he sat with the Saxon leader and they agreed to a truce.

"The dragon warrior was twenty-eight, as I am, and unmarried, as I am. The Saxon king offered his daughter to the dragon as bride in a show of good faith and to unite the clans, but the young warrior did not want an unwilling bride. He made a command. He would marry from the Saxons as the truce demanded but whoever he wed must be willing to join him of her own free will. He stayed with the Saxons for a time to find a mate. That was when he fell in love with a handmaid and asked for her. The maid agreed and they were joined. Since then, every twenty years there must be another woman who is willing to join in marriage with a dragonman to keep the truce alive."

"And you think I am the lass? And I am to what? Marry you?" My heart was telling me it was so, but my mind rebelled.

Aodhfionn took a deep breath and took my hand. "I would take care of you, lass," he said. "You would want for nothing. I am to be king. You, my queen. At least consider your position in society. You told me yourself your clan has not accepted you. Would you not try to be with another?" I stood and began to pace in front of the cave entrance.

"I am a witch. Do you want to be married to someone they will burn at the stake like they did my mother?" I couldn't believe the words were out of my mouth. Aodhfionn's eyes narrowed and he stood suddenly. I backed away, but my heel caught on a rock. I would have gone tumbling down the cliff had he not caught me and pulled me to him.

He pressed me to his chest as if I was his wife, his woman. His to comfort. But I was not his. And I would *not* be his. Pushing away from him, I broke his hold and turned to scurry down the mountain's face. Aodhfionn's voice echoed behind me but it wasn't until I nearly tripped did I hear the roar of his dragon. Suddenly, my stomach lurched and the ground beneath me was gone. His large talon was wrapped around my middle as he carried me, not away, but to the ground.

Finally, when we landed, I tried to run, but he shifted so fast I could not move. He grasped my arms and held me to him.

I tried to fight but instead of coming close enough to me as he had before, he kept his knees, groin and any other easily damageable parts away from the reach of my legs.

"Let me go!" I shouted.

"Look at me, lass," he demanded. I stopped at the sheer power in his voice. "Would you shame me by denying me in front of my own clan? I donnae ask anything of you. And I certainly will make no demands on you that you find so abhorrent. All I ask is that you donnae shame me before my clan and my family. My father is a proud man and he will not take kindly to the Lewis breaking the truce. If you want to save that clan of yours, then do as I ask and I promise you, once this is over, you will be released, free and untouched. But let me give my father this before the clan and when I can speak with him alone, I will explain."

I stared at him. It was quite the promise, considering the tales I had heard from the married women. The men took what they wanted, and it mattered little if they were not willing. My uncle forced himself on his new bride on their wedding night. She told me horror stories. But something about the man before me told me he was nothing like the men in my clan.

Slowly, I nodded. "How long?"

"Give me three months," he begged. "Once I speak with my father today, I will tell him everything. But do this one thing for me, lass and I swear I will make no designs on you. I beg you, be calm. We may need to marry for the image of the clan, share a chamber even, but I swear to you on the lives of my mother and sister, I will never touch you unless you ask."

"I will not ask," I stated. The marriage bed held no appeal to me. But if I was expected to pretend, I needed to be sure, my image and honor remained intact.

"Would you shame me by joining others in their bed?"

He released me and took a step back. His face betrayed the wound I had just inflicted with my words. "Do you think me a knave? When I pledge to you before the others here, I will be true to you. Even though you deny me, I will not take nor invite others to my bed. I will be your husband in all ways save one. I would never dishonor my father's house by bedding another while I am married. So long as you give me no concern that you have taken another to our bed, then I swear to you I will be faithful to you."

I breathed easier. "You have my word," I swore.

"Good, now let us go to my father. Please, while we are among my clan, pretend to like me," he said.

If I was honest with myself, I did like him, or rather his warrior spoke to mine. He held his honor to standards I appreciated. He would keep his word; of that I had no question. But the thought of freedom, of being able to leave this land and go somewhere where my talents were accepted and not frowned upon, was tempting. To be free of my uncle's tyranny was the true goal and Aodhfionn had made that possible.

My own response to his presence was confusing. But as he offered his arm to me, I slowly slid my hand through the crook of his elbow. We walked toward the keep together in silence. My heart began pounding with concern. All of this was foreign to me and I did not know what to expect. I only knew Aodhfionn would be by my side and all would be well.

Finn

I shook my head at my dragon's internal grumbling. I had promised not to touch this woman who made my skin light up with a fire even my dragon hadn't felt before. The beast was screaming at me inside my head, telling me how much of a fool I was and all I could do was take the beating. My head would ache later with the strength used to keep the beast at bay.

We walked in silence and I had to stop myself from speaking to distract from the noise in my head. What I wouldn't give to be inside that head of hers. What was she thinking? I could hear her heart speed up as we neared the doors of the keep and I worried. The guard opened the heavy iron doors for us to enter and I listened for any subtle change in her breathing.

Brigid's loud gasp made me turn. She was gazing at the ninety-foot-high tower and the two baby dragons fighting each other high up inside the round building.

"My nephews," I whispered. "Little terrors but I love them."

"Are they always in dragon form as children?"

"No, we learn to shift at a young age. They enjoy being in their dragon forms, but they can be human too."

She nodded and her eyes darted around the great hall. Nothing ostentatious, my father prided himself on his fair treatment of his clan. It was a tradition I hoped to uphold when I was king. Brigid walked beside me, but I felt her slow down as she took in the sights. Indeed, to a human or even a dragon seeing it for the first time, it was a terrifyingly beautiful sight. My father, the great dragon king stood on the dais holding and cooing to the newest addition to our family, my niece. Still a babe, she was such a treasure and not only because female dragons were few.

"Aodhfionn!" My father called, his jovial nature with all in his clan but especially with me, shown through as he passed his granddaughter off to her mother, my sister-by-mating. "And this must be your lovely bride!"

Brigid's grip on my arm increased but she bowed to the king and kept her eyes downcast.

"Aye, Da', this is Brigid of Clan Lewis."

"Och, come over here and give me a hug, lass," my father laughed. "No need to stand on ceremony! You are my new daughter!" Brigid's eyes rose and I saw determination reflected in their blue depths. I let go of her hand and my father engulfed her in a hug. Pulling back, he continued. "If this lad of mine gives you any trouble, you let me know. I'll sort him out in no time." My father ruffled my hair as if I were still a lad. "Come and sit with me. You must be hungry after such a long journey. Come. Bring food and wine for your new lady!" My father called to the serving women. "Now, I know this is all new and probably a little foreign to you. But I want you to feel as comfortable as possible. Are there any questions you may have for us? Speak freely, my dear."

"Dragons are real?" She blurted out. I closed my eyes as I felt my father's snap to me.

Chapter Six

Brigid

What did I just say? Aodhfionn asked me to at least pretend and I had let my awe and surprise come out. My mother always told me I was like my father in that regard, always speaking my mind. But I bit my tongue in that instance. I saw the king's brown eyes flash to Aodhfionn, and I couldn't help but look away and try to salvage the conversation.

"What I mean is... It is all so sudden, and I did not realize how *real* you are in the genuine sense. I always thought you were larger than life and so grand. Forgive me, I am nervous meeting such a great king." I was rambling, I knew, but I couldn't stop. I hoped a tip to his self-pride might alleviate some anger.

The king's eyes pulled from his son and back to me. He reached forward and patted my hand.

"Well, that's neither here nor there, lass," he said. "Tell

me about yourself."

"I am a…" I began, then my eyes turned to Aodhfionn. "A healer, your majesty." I looked back.

"Och, *majesty* is far too formal," he smiled. "My name is Edan please call me that."

"You are too kind," I replied. He grinned and glanced over at his son.

"Was your mother a healer as well?" he asked me.

"Aye," my voice choked. My mother's memory was still painful. "But she is gone."

"Och lass, I am sorry," Edan replied. "Did you know her?"

"Aye, she was killed when I was a young lass," I answered.

"I am so verra sorry," he said.

"Tell him what you told me, Brigid. You have nothing to fear," Aodhfionn spoke softly.

"Of course not!" the king cried. "Tell me anything, my dear."

I took a deep breath and looked at Aodhfionn. I don't know why, but even after only knowing him half a day, he gave me comfort.

"I am a healer, your maj… Edan," I corrected. "But my clan feared me thinking my practices were more… witchcraft. My mother… was burned at the stake for such a slight."

I could feel the king shake beside me. I raised my head, proud still knowing who my father was but not wanting to see the anger and hatred in the king's eyes. Instead of fierce loathing and yelling, the king spoke low as he gently took my hand.

"You poor poor dear," he replied. "I am so very sorry for all you have been through. I can only imagine. And to still have the grace, pride, and respect you carry… that is strength indeed. But now, you must freshen up, I am sure you would like a nice warm bath before supper is served. We will be toasting my eldest son and his new bride."

Try as I might, I could find no animosity in his voice. I looked over at Aodhfionn who smiled and soon a young woman came up to the front of the dais.

"Sara will be your personal chambermaid. If that is acceptable to you."

"I am not used to such extravagance," I admitted. Finn cleared his throat softly. "But I am grateful to you, Sara." I spoke to the young woman. She curtsied. Standing, I thanked the king for speaking with me. They both stood as I left. Looking back over my shoulder, I saw both men watching me, but the look on Aodhfionn's face was one that would haunt me. He looked almost wounded I had left without a word to him. Why, I couldn't fathom... but he had been nothing but kind to me. Smiling slightly, I liked how his eyes lightened and flashed to dragon slits and back. Soon, he was out of my sight and I was led to a beautiful room two flights up.

Sara opened the door and I took it all in. It was the largest room I had ever seen, soaring ceilings, deep rich mahogany furnishings, a large bearskin lay before the lit fire in the massive hearth, and a bed fit for a king. The room was elegant and the dancing white fire in the fireplace lent to the majesty of it all.

"This will be your chamber, my lady for the two nights until the ceremony," the young woman, Sara explained. "After that your things will move down the hall into his highness' room. It is the family's wing. The king and queen share the chamber three doors down from you."

"Together?" I questioned. My uncle never shared a chamber with his wife, either of them.

The young chambermaid giggled. "Och, aye," she answered. "They are as in love today as they were when my mum was chambermaid. And of course, for you it will be early days in your marriage but even after a whelp or two is born you will still want to remain with the prince."

I said nothing.

"The princess's and princes' rooms are down the hall too," she went on. "The king's and queen's solars are upstairs."

"How many?" I asked as she motioned for me to sit at the dressing table.

"How many siblings?" she clarified as she went to pull the pot over the fire. It still glowed white. I recognized it as Aodhfionn's fire from when he breathed the flames in the cave.

"Five, my lady. There is Aodhfionn, the eldest as you ken. Then Cahal, best stay clear of him, my lady. He is a broody one." Her eyes grew wide. "Please, donnae tell anyone I said that." At my smile and agreement, she continued. "Teyrnon is next. He's a handsome devil and a flirt," she giggled as her cheeks reddened. "Then Bearcbhan, he is mated to Sybine and they have three whelps. Tahra is the youngest. She must be about your age, my lady."

I nodded, contemplating all she had told me as I watched her pour the steaming water into the large copper tub standing proudly by the fire.

As a healer, I prided myself on my memory and ability to remember names after only meeting once. The young woman looked up at me and placed her hands on her hips.

"Now, my lady, let us get you comfortable and into this lovely bath." She sprinkled some oils into the water and the smell of lavender and sage drifted to my nostrils.

"That smells heavenly," I said. Only then did I realize how sore my body was and how tired I felt. "You will stay, I hope, Sara? I am so tired. I worry I may fall asleep."

"Of course, my lady! But I will be quiet. Mum always says I jabber on."

I smiled. "How old are you, Sara?"

"Sixteen," she beamed.

"I think we will become great friends."

"I would be honored, my lady."

"One more thing, Sara," I stood as she came to help me untie my dress. "When we are alone, please call me Brigid. I understand the need for the *my lady* when we have others near us, but I ask you to call me Brigid."

"Oh, I donnae ken, my lady," she said, her already wide eyes growing even wider. "That is most inappropriate."

"Just when we are alone, Sara, please."

She took a deep breath. "I suppose it would nae hurt and so long as I have your permission... verra well, Brigid," she giggled. "I like you verra much."

"And I you, Sara," I smiled.

"Now, let us get you into the water, then I will call the other ladies. They will provide you with a gown until your own arrive."

I doubted I would ever have any of my own things arrive. My uncle certainly would not send anything and Aodhfionn would not go either. Tears pricked my eyes as I thought of Lir. Without me there, he would starve. Leaning my head back on the rim of the bath, I forced my tears to stop. I would get back to him. I may have promised three months but Lir was counting on me. I would find a way to get him. If I had to force one of the dragons to take me to him at knife point, I would do it. They looked upon me as their future queen after all. I would find a way.

Chapter Seven

Finn

My dragon did not like the look in her eye as she left the great hall. She had promised me three months, but I was unsure if she would stay. My beast moved just beneath my skin, eager to have his mate by his side but when she looked back at me and smiled, my dragon calmed.

"Leave us," my father called to the guards around the great hall. I could no longer hear my nephews' dragons above us. We were alone. "Tell me what happened, lad."

Huffing a sigh, I turned to the fire and stared down into the yellow flames. Yellow and red. Unlike my own, this was my father's fire. Mine was white as my name indicated.

I did not speak for a time but soon felt my father touch my arm with a cup of whisky in his hand. I took it and clinked the glass to his. Our forges, deep below the keep and throughout the clan's lands, were lit with dragon fire, hot enough to cure glass.

"Let's sit." We sat at the chairs before the fire, sipping whiskey. "You already care for her," Da' finally continued.

"I confess I do," I answered. "But anyone would, when you hear what I saw and her story."

"Tell me," Da' ordered.

"She is a warrior. Never have I seen a human female fight so powerfully. I would swear she is dragonborn if I could not scent the human," I touched the thin white scar still on my chest where her wee knife had broken my flesh. I looked over at my father. He waited, simply drinking his whisky. "When I arrived on Lewis land, I circled, watching. I saw the laird and his clan. I saw Brigid. She was shouting at him. Apparently, he led her father and other warriors to their death. I heard her call him uncle, but I believe it was by her mother, they are related."

"You have a point, I know, lad," he stopped me. "You can tell me all of this after that. What is it you are trying to delay telling me?"

I huffed. "You always could read me far too well, Da'." My father merely smiled and raised the glass to his lips. "My point is... they did not give her a choice."

My father started and leaned forward. "What?" he was horrified. "You mean that sweet lass has no idea what is asked of her?"

"None," I answered.

"All right, now go back and tell me everything, lad," he said.

Sighing, I nodded and we both sat back in the chairs before the fire. I continued and finished with the conversation Brigid and I had on top of the mountain. My father stared at me for a long while, no emotion on his face.

Finally, he spoke low. "That Lewis bastard has broken

the treaty," he spat.

"Aye, but I ask you to stay your fire, Da'. Brigid is willing to become my wife in all ways save one and in three months, I will be able to release her."

"You would give up physical relations for her?" My father asked delicately.

"They mean little in the grand scheme," I answered.

"Finn," Da' began. "I love you but I cannae see you hurt like that. If you already care for her, and if your dragon claims her..."

"He will nae," I stated.

"You said you would be a husband to her in all ways save one, that means you would die for her. That is no way to live. And what if your fears are realized and she finds a way to leave? I will not have my first born mocked and ridiculed nor will I have you take another after her simply for the convenience of producing an heir. You have no control over your dragon's claim."

"I am saying, she will have the protection of my house as well as my body," I explained. "But I will not marry her in truth. When the time comes, and the time will come, she wishes to leave, she will leave with my full blessing, untouched. Perhaps then she will have an opportunity to find a good marriage."

"You would do that for her?" he asked. I could tell my father did not believe me and I understood why. Up until a couple years ago, I was as randy as Kai.

"As you would for mother," I answered.

"But your mother and I love each other," he stated.

"Not at first you did not," I reminded him of the arranged marriage their fathers negotiated. "Do you tell me you would have done naught for her even then? I ken that is false."

My father sighed and nodded his head. "Aye you are right. But forgive me lad, you are a very physical dragon," he went on. "I myself have caught you in a couple compromising positions." He chuckled.

"Aye, I remember well," I answered. "But I will do this, and I ask you to not tell anyone, save perhaps Ma, of my plan. I donnae want the clan to shun Brigid. She has been shunned enough. I would have her loved as our future queen. For however long that may be."

"I give you my word, lad. No one shall hear of this plan, and I commend you for your valor."

"'Tis a trait I inherited," I smiled at him.

"Och," he waved me off, but I could see the sparkle in his eye.

"And as for your fear of her leaving, I will go back and find her. But there must be a reason. She mentioned the name Lir."

"A lover? A child?" Da' asked.

"Nay, she is a maiden, a warrior maiden but a maiden, nonetheless. It could be something else. I will ask. If that is the reason she wants to leave, I will go get it."

"No one is to go to Lewis lands without my blessing."

"Da'," I reasoned.

He held up his hand. "Find out. We will discuss it then. Now, 'tis time for you to join your bride in preparing for the dinner. Warn her about the ceremony, lad. For those who have never heard of us, it will be an interesting experience."

"I will warn her," I answered. "I donnae want my bride running out the door as soon as she enters. Even if it is her greatest wish. Not yet anyway."

"Aye, we donnae want that. What of the bedding ceremony, lad? How will you explain that to the males?"

"I will ask for privacy that night," I answered. "And a small finger prick should do the trick."

"Aye and I will decree, as my son, there is no need of witnesses. If they question, then I will volunteer to be there. Hopefully, she is not averse to sharing a room with you," he said.

"Nay, I have spoken to her. I will offer to sleep elsewhere besides the bed," I explained.

"Well lad, I wish you well," he raised his cup and drank it down. "But I do believe Lewis needs to be dealt with."

"Aye, I agree, but give me a couple months to figure out a plan, I beg of you."

"You ken I donnae like anyone flouting our laws."

"Aye, nor do I and I am your warrior in this and all. But I beg of you, I am to take over this clan as your decree has given me eight months. I ask you, allow me to think of a way to punish the clan without hurting my bride's love of her people. Though she has no love for her uncle, she loves the people. She will never forgive me."

My father stared at me for a long time then finally nodded. "You have proven yourself always to be my champion and choice to succeed me. But in this, my lad, I am proud and honored to be called your father."

Those words did something to me and as I raised myself up in my chair, I nodded once at him in thanks.

"Now go. Dress in your finest, and we will have a celebration. I trust she is not averse to kissing you," he stated.

The kiss. I had forgotten about the kiss. The traditional ceremonial kiss before the clan staking my claim on her as my bride. I would need to beg an audience with her before dinner and explain the situation. I hoped she would not secret away a knife and try to stab me again. I chuckled to myself. Perhaps she would grant me this bit of tradition.

Brigid

After being bathed, brushed, pampered, sprayed, combed, plaited, dressed, and powdered, I was looking at the image reflected in the shined silver plate before me. The dress was deep green, complimenting my red hair and matching Aodhfionn's eyes. The women all spoke to me about him and how wonderful a king he would make. There was even some innuendo about his skills in other areas as well. I promised him I would not tell anyone of our arrangement and smiled at what the women said.

Just as the last wayward strain of hair was placed, a knock at the door drew our attention. Sara went to the door and opened it.

"If she is ready may I have a moment?" I recognized his voice already.

"Aye, my prince," she answered bowing and stepping to the side.

I stood and his eyes fell on me. They lit with a sort of fire I had not seen before. It was as if his dragon's fire raged behind his eyes. It was too hot, and I looked down. He wore a kilt of green, yellow, and red that rested just at his knees. A longer piece fell behind him, with a sash crossing his chest and secured with a brooch. He was freshly shaven. His brown hair was washed and flopped about him; the curls made my hands ache to run through them. I clenched my fists to stop the odd behavior. He wore a large ring on his right hand. The red precious gem glistened under a dragon's silhouette cut from gold and wrapped on top of the stone.

It was then I realized, we were alone. The women had left while I was staring at the dragonman before me.

"You look beautiful, lass," he said softly.

"I thank you," I looked down. "You look very handsome. I thank you and your father for these gifts." I gestured to the dress and wine resting on the table. "'Tis far too much."

"'Tis not enough," he answered. "After everything you went through..." Shaking his head, he sighed. "I should tell you; my father knows of our... arrangement. I did not think it wise to keep him in the dark."

"I understand and I am sorry for any difficulty it has caused you both."

"Nae difficulty," he answered. "May I shut the door?"

Nodding, I agreed and sat back at my dressing table. I would need to be alone with him soon, what did it matter when? The door shut, Aodhfionn walked over to me. He indicated the bed asking if he could sit. I nodded and he sat facing me. I turned to him and he locked eyes with me.

"I am sorry to corner you in your bedchamber, lass. But when I was speaking with my father, he reminded me of something. I find I need to ask your permission." I said nothing. "Tonight, there is a ceremony, a short one, for the clan to see you as my new bride. The wedding will be the day after tomorrow but tonight, after my father makes the announcement, the clan will pound on the table. That is their request to see a kiss."

My throat closed and I forced my swallow. "They will expect it. If you give me your permission, I will make it a short one but there is always the question of if they will be satisfied. If you would allow me to kiss you in a way I know the clan will approve of, I promise you I will not do so again." I waited a moment. A kiss was intimate, but not as much as an act of love making. I had seen many kiss in my clan, either at weddings, after battle, or as an invitation. Could I kiss him? Would he find my lack of experience abhorrent? "Have you ever been kissed before, lass?" He prompted.

I did not know if I could speak. My throat was closed, and it felt like hands were around my neck. It suddenly grew warm. Forcing my mind and body to be as one, I grounded myself, looked up into his inviting green eyes, and pulled on every strength I had. Finally, I spoke the truth. "Once."

Finn

Gods, the female is a marvel. I watched her war with herself. After everything she went through that day, the fear of being burned alive, to being stolen by a dragon and told that I was her mate, then to be forced into a situation she was unable to control, she was still able to focus and give me an answer. It was selfish of me to ask if she had been kissed before, but I needed to know who had been near what was mine.

"Once," she answered. "A soft peck as a lass, from a friend before he left to be fostered."

"It was not the knave that tricked you was it?" I demanded. She looked away. My fists ached. I wanted to fly over there and challenge both he and her uncle for the bastards they were. One who should have protected her as kith and kin and the other who claimed to be her friend. When I turned to her, her eyes were on my balled fist. My stomach dropped. Had someone ever hit her? I saw the truth in her eyes but also the determination, a mask she wore hiding her true feelings. I relaxed my hand and crouched low in front of her.

"I want you to feel comfortable with me, lass," I said. "I am not angry at you. I am upset at the pain your clan inflicted upon you. I would never strike you."

She nodded but did not look at me.

"Brigid," I called. Finally, her eyes rose to mine. Kneeling before her, I took out my dirk strapped to my arm and placed the tip before my heart, the hilt out to her. She straightened and looked at me. "I swear on the iron I hold, if I ever raise my hand to you, this blade will pierce my heart. I pledge if you ever need me, I will be there. If I ever break your trust or this bond, I ask this dirk pierce my heart. I am your servant. My pledge is my bond. If you ever need me, I will be there. I swear it to you."

She stared at me for a moment, then, "we're not really marrying, Aodhfionn."

"We will be married in all ways but one," I reminded her. "And I will not have my wife want for anything. Even after you have left."

Studying me, she finally took the hilt of the dagger, released it from my grip, and moved the point from my chest. Raising it to her lips, she kissed the iron hilt and looked at me.

"You have my permission to do as you see fit this evening," she said. "If you believe a strong kiss is what your clan would want to see, then you may kiss me however you desire." I breathed a sigh of relief and chose to ignore my beast's jubilant reaction.

Taking my dirk back from her wee hand, I kissed the same spot and lowered it to the sheath.

"Aodhfionn," she said.

"Finn, lass," I replied.

"Finn," she acquiesced. "In my clan there's a tradition on the wedding night. The men of the clan want to make sure the marriage is... consummated. Do you have that here?"

"Aye," I answered. "But I have spoken to my father and he has agreed to suspend the tradition. As king, he will claim that me being his first-born son, no witness is needed. If anyone should ask, he will offer to be witness and no one would dare question the king." She nodded and bit her lower lip. I fought the urge to kiss it.

A knock at the door made her jump and a small screech emitted from her lips. I went to the door and opened it. One of my father's guards stood there and called us to dinner. Turning back to my bride, I offered my hand to her. She slipped her slim fingers onto my palm and I tucked them around my arm. Together, we walked out of the room and down the hallway to the steps leading to the Great Hall.

Chapter Eight

Finn

As soon as we reached the Great Hall, cheers erupted, and Brigid leaned further into me. The impressive sight of my clan standing and cheering for us as we walked in, would cause any human to be nervous. Dragons were large. Each man in the clan was well over the human height and the women towered over Brigid. But my human, after a moment of nerves, pulled herself up to her full height, coming to my shoulder, and stood by my side; regal. Pride flared in my veins as I looked down at her, then a sort of pain that she would never in truth be mine came over me. Covering her hand on my arm, I squeezed it and we locked eyes. She smiled slightly. We walked to my father's table on the dais where my three brothers and my sister-in-law stood to greet us.

Watching my two unattached kin, I pulled Brigid closer to me. Their hungry gazes caused my inner dragon to demand a fight. Suppressing the beast's instinct to protect his mate, I guided Brigid up the stairs, and she curtsied to my father, who greeted her warmly and offered a seat beside him. When she looked back at me, I pushed my youngest brother out of the way, and took a seat beside her, ignoring Bearcbhan's chuckle.

"Allow me, my dear to introduce my three younger sons," my father began. "This is Cahal my second born, Teyrnon my third and Bearcbhan my youngest."

"And slowest," Teyrnon teased.

"And best with the lasses," Bearcbhan replied pulling his wife, Sybine into him and giving her a passionate kiss.

"Not while I'm eating," Cahal grumbled.

"It is a pleasure to meet you. I believe I saw your sons earlier," Brigid said addressing my youngest brother.

"Aye, most likely. Da' lets them shift and play in the rafters. Wee devils but they're mine," Bearcbhan grinned proudly.

"Are they twins?" she asked.

"Aye, and the gods help me, they drive me senseless," his wife spoke up. Brigid laughed.

"I believe it," she said. "And is the wee lass I saw, also yours?"

"Aye, our darling," she replied. "Her grandda' is quite smitten with her." Sybine beamed at my father.

"She is my joy," Da' said.

"I believe you also have a younger sister?"

"Aye, we do, lass," Bearcbhan stated. "Tahra, she is in Ireland with our mum at the moment, but we expect them back soon."

"Do either of you have mates?" Brigid asked my other two brothers.

"Not yet, lass," Teyrnon stated. "Why? You offering?"

"Teyrnon," my father and I snapped together. Brigid gripped my hand, stopping me. I looked at her and she smiled. Looking Teyrnon straight in the eye, she spoke.

"I am pleased to say I am already spoken for by your brother, Teyrnon. And if the gossip of the ladies in my chamber was anything to go on, my wedding night and all nights after, will be well blessed with Aodhfionn in my bed. I donnae think his... *younger* brother would have anywhere near his... skills."

All at the table were silent. I tried to hide my shock and surprise, but I failed miserably. It sounded as if she truly believed what she said, but by the gods the fierceness in her voice and the passion in her eyes as she stood up to my brother, made me grin and pull her close. She looked over at me as I tipped her chin up. Without thinking, I lowered my mouth to hers and took her lips in a kiss. As soon as my lips touched hers, my sanity returned for a split second and I pulled away, ready to apologize for taking such a liberty, but her hands gripped my tunic and pulled me back to her.

Brigid

Why I pulled Finn back to me when he pulled away, I did not know. All I could think of was how right he felt. We hardly knew each other but already he had made me care for him by being the finest man I had ever met. He deepened the kiss, but when we heard someone groan in disgust, Finn pulled back. His eyes flashed to his dragon slits then back to the round of his human, confused.

"Well now, I suppose that would work for the clan," his father said. My eyes looked out to the Great Hall to see everyone staring at us. Immediately, I felt my cheeks flame red and I looked down. All my warrior training had not prepared me for how to handle the situation I now found myself.

"Perhaps the time has come *before* the meal to make the announcement." Edan rose from his seat and, with a booming voice, he addressed the clan. "My eldest son has chosen to participate in the treaty we have with the Lewis clan. As you know, every twenty years one of our dragon men receives the gift of his future bride. I am very grateful for this tradition since my mother was one such a lass," he looked at me and winked. "Now my son has followed in my father's footsteps and agreed to take a human lass as his bride and made an excellent choice. I ask you raise your cups to their happiness and allow me to introduce Lady Brigid, my son's bride and your future queen!" He raised his cup and the clan followed. They cried something in Gaelic and drank. Then the pounding started on the table. Aodhfionn stood and locked eyes with me as he offered his hand.

Accepting, I took his hand and stood. We faced the clan but before he kissed me, his eyes asked permission. I nodded. If I was honest with myself, I wanted to have his kiss again.

Chapter Nine

Finn

The dinner passed without much trouble. My brother Cahal eyed my bride with a suspicious gaze. I would need to keep an eye on him. I refused to have Brigid feel uncomfortable. She was a master at conversation with my brothers, father, and sister-in-law. I looked forward to introducing her to my mother and sister. Once the festivities died down, Brigid covered a yawn and I took her hand from under the table.

"We could be excused if you wish it, lass," I whispered once she looked up at me. "You have had a long day."

"'Tis the truth I am tired," she admitted. "But I donnae want to disrupt tradition. The ladies told me this afternoon I am to stay until the end." My heart swelled with pride. Even after everything she went through, she still wanted to keep to our traditions.

"That is true but only because the announcement would have been made at the end. Since our announcement was made earlier, we can leave at our leisure."

"Truly?" she whispered.

"Aye," I answered smiling at the hope in her eyes. "Come with me." I took her hand and stood, turning to my father. "Forgive me for interrupting you, Da', but Brigid and I are tired. Considering the week we have before us, I believe a good sleep is necessary."

"Aye, 'tis, lad," he answered. "My best to you both and I shall see you tomorrow."

"I thank you for your hospitality, sire," Brigid said with a curtsey.

"Och, you are family now, lass," he grinned. "Go now. Finn will take care of you."

Cahal scoffed and looked away. My eyes drifted to my brother and then back to Da'. My father nodded and leaned over to him, whispering something in his ear. My brother blinked a few times and looked down. My father pulled away and shared a glance with me. Nodding my thanks, I took Brigid's hand, we walked to the stairs.

Brigid

Finn escorted me up the steps of the keep and down the hall. Once we were at the door to my room, I turned to look at him.

"Can you tell me what to expect at the ceremony? I am supposed to know what to do and I do not want to let anyone know that I do not. Nor make you look less in the eyes of your clan."

"Of course," Finn answered, a strange look flashed in his eyes, but it was gone before I could study it. "Let us go inside and away from any ears."

I nodded. We entered the dark room and I shivered. The fire had died down to embers as we were in the Great Hall. Immediately, Finn went to the fireplace. In the darkness, I could not see what happened, but the fire was lit with a sort of white flame and instantly the room warmed. He turned to the window and lowered the furs, making sure they were tight against the windowpane. The room started to warm, and I began to relax. Finn walked back to me and spoke low.

"If you wish for the door to remain open, I will not shut it, but perhaps, for this conversation, a closed door would be best." I nodded in agreement and he shut the heavy oak door but left it unbarred. "You are chilled, lass. Shall we sit before the fire?"

"I thank you, I am well," I answered and took the plaid which hung over the chair and wrapped it around my shoulders. We sat together in the two large chairs beside the fire.

"Tell me something, lass," Finn started. "How did you know about my sister?"

I paused a moment, my eyes moving to the door.

"Sara told you things?" he asked. I nodded. "What did she say?"

"She will not be in any trouble, aye?" I would defend Sara against any retribution. She only told me what I needed to know.

"Not unless she insulted my father or mother," he answered. That was reasonable, but I wanted him to know, she was fiercely loyal.

"Nay, she would never. She is loyal to you and the king and queen."

"Good, then what did she tell you?"

"Merely that you would be a great king. Teyrnon is a flirt and Bearcbhan and Sybine have three children. Then Tahra is the youngest, about my age."

"And Cahal?"

I swallowed. "Please, she meant no disrespect."

"I understand, she will be in no trouble."

I looked down and sighed. "She said to stay away from him. He is broody. Please, she told me in confidence."

"I am glad she told you. And I agree with her sentiments. Please, keep away from him. He wasn't always like this, and I hold one day he will return to his former self. But I have little hope of that happening."

"What happened to cause him to become so..."

"Angry?"

My brows furrowed and I shook my head. "I do not see anger. I see sadness and a sort of pain. If there is anything I can do to help him... a cure of some kind. I am a healer."

"Aye, but I donnae think even your extraordinary talents could cure him of his pain. It is an internal pain."

"A pain of the heart," I surmised.

"Aye."

"I am sorry for him. I ken well pains of the heart. Perhaps I could speak with him. One broken heart to another."

"Nay, I will nae allow it. For your own safety, lass. He is dangerous. He does nae mean to be, I am sure, but more than one person has been hurt by his sudden outbursts. I will nae have you hurt."

"I can take care of myself, Finn."

"Aye and you have done well but you are nay alone any longer. I will take care of you. I will have your word on this, Brigid. Stay away from my brother."

I debated for a long moment. Shamefully, I wondered if Cahal was a way for me to leave and go back to my home but the thought of leaving Finn and the place I felt welcome and cared for, ached more than I wanted. But I had to leave and soon. Lir depended on me. He had been by himself all day and I could only pray he was unharmed. The idea he could be starving made my heart lurch and tears formed in my eyes.

"Lass?" I heard. Looking up, Finn's face filled with horror and he knelt to the ground. "Forgive me, I did nae mean to cause your tears. 'Tis only, I ken Cahal and I donnae want you hurt."

"Nay, 'tis no' that," tears flowed, and I hated the show of weakness.

"Then what?" he begged. "Tell me, lass and if it is within my power to help and stay your tears, I will do all I can."

I swiped at my tears, but they refused to stop. My throat was painful from the lump that continued to grow.

"I miss Lir," I finally got out. "He'll die if I donnae get to him. Please, Finn, let me go home. You can tell everyone I was not pleasing to you, that I was not a good woman, anything you desire. I donnae care, but please, let me go home."

His face contorted in pain and he wrapped his arms around me. I found I rather liked his embrace, it was soft, loving, and gentle.

"Lass, I would do anything for you. But I cannae let you go without starting a war. Dragons are possessive and they have claimed you as one of their own. If they found out you were not willing and I let you go before mating you and therefore the treaty is broken, they will move heaven and earth to win you back and war would come to both our clans. Please understand, I will let you go with a full heart, but I must beg you, for the sake of your clan's lives, stay with me a little longer."

"I cannae. Lir will die!"

"Who is Lir?" he asked softly.

"My deerhound," I answered. Finn breathed a sigh of... relief? I did not understand. An image of the sweet pup's old man face with his grey and white fur and short beard came to mind and tears welled in my eyes again. "I will probably never see him again. He's all alone and I couldn't protect him when they came to take me to the keep."

"I am sure he is well," Finn said. "Deerhounds are a strong breed."

"Aye, but he's the gentlest giant I know," I replied. "I cannae be without him. I donnae know if I'll be able to sleep without him beside me. He will die."

"He will not. I give you my word. You must get your rest, lass," he urged.

"I cannae go through with this, Finn," I confessed. "I..."

"I know," he answered. "If it wasn't essential for the clan to think the treaty is still active, I would never put you through this, lass. Do you trust me?"

I nodded unsure as to why, but I knew in my heart, I trusted him. He would see it right.

"I pledged to you right here before we went down for dinner. I pledged to be your protector and I hold to that. You are strong, lass, one of the things I admire most about you. You have had to be strong for so long. Let someone else help you, carry your burdens. You are not alone any longer. Let me in. Let me help."

"I have held myself up for so long, I donnae know if I can let someone else in," I said.

"Try?" he offered. "I am not asking to be more than a friend, a confidant to you. Take me into your trust, lass. That is all I ask."

After a moment, I nodded and whispered. "I trust you, Finn. And I will stay here. I will not attempt to leave. But please, if I mean anything to you, save my deerhound."

"Think no more on that, lass. He's as good as saved."

I smiled at him and nodded. "Thank you."

"Now, would you like some spiced wine?"

Shaking my head. I was drained both emotionally and physically. "Tea?" I asked.

"Aye, that sounds good," he went to the door and opened it, disappearing for a moment. "Sara will bring us some." He stated, walking back to me.

"Finn?" I started after he sat.

"Aye?"

"Teyrnon said your mother and sister are in Ireland. Why?"

He smiled sweetly. "She is visiting her family."

"She is Irish?" at his nod, I continued. "Is that why you have an Irish name?"

"Aye," he answered. "My mother is from a beautiful place in the west of Ireland. She should be here tomorrow."

"The ceremony is the day after tomorrow? Tell me what to expect?"

"Aye, it's an interesting thing to see." Before he could continue, there was a knock at the door. Finn answered it and carried the tea tray back to where we were sitting. He placed it on the table and poured two cups. "How do you like your tea?"

"Just the way it is," I answered. "I have never had it any other way."

"No cream or honey?" He asked.

I shook my head, too embarrassed to admit I was too poor to have anything other than goat's milk. His hand came up to my cheek and the soft touch made me turn to look at him.

"Donnae turn those beautiful blue eyes from me, lass," he said. "Talk to me. I render no judgement."

"I..." my throat was dry as he held my gaze, an emotion I could not name invaded my heart. "I have never had tea any other way. I could not afford it."

"You have not had honey?" He asked. I shook my head. I was terrified of bees and had never drawn near a hive to collect its nectar. "Let me make up my tea the way I enjoy it and you try it. If you prefer your way, then none the wiser. Will you try it?" I nodded. I watched as he measured out the golden sweet honey. Once finished, he offered it to me. I slowly took a sip of the hot liquid. Sweetness hit my tongue, but I did not appreciate the taste and my face must have betrayed my opinion. "Nay?" he chuckled. "Well then, perhaps this will taste better." He offered the other cup.

"I am sorry," I said.

"No need to apologize, lass," he replied. "Now drink your tea and let us speak of the ceremony."

Chapter Ten

Finn

She was asleep. I should have left but I could not stop watching her. She had her tea. We had spoken at length about the ceremony and we fell silent enjoying each other's company. The fire still burned white hot and was not likely to go out any time soon. Dragon fire stayed lit for a long time. I had disciplined my dragon to be able to breathe a bit of fire even in human form.

She had returned the teacup to the tray and had slowly closed her eyes. I watched her sleep, thinking how much I enjoyed, not only her company but her fire and spirit. Holding her as she cried that evening had done something to my heart. I was more determined than ever to show her I would be a good husband to her, in every sense. And after the kiss... I refused to let my heart hope. She had all but admitted she was trying to find a way to escape. Standing silently, I walked over to her and carefully lifted her. She hummed but rolled into me. Her head burrowed into my chest and she sighed. For a moment, I did not let her go. I reveled in the feeling of her in my arms. I simply stared down at her and then she slowly opened her eyes.

If she saw me or knew where she was, I was not sure. But she did not fight, she simply gazed up at me and smiled softly, then fell back asleep. I needed to leave. I had promised her I could restrain but her smile made me question my resolve. Gently setting her down on her bed, I went to the door and opened it. Calling for Sara to assist her out of her clothes, I gave strict instructions that she not wake her. Then, I left the room and headed downstairs.

The Great Hall was littered with drunk dragons, all piled on each other. That was a tame sight compared to what would happen the night of the wedding. Dragons took weddings very seriously and the celebrations after were legendary. Picking my way around them, I walked out the back entrance. The cold air did wonders for my overheated skin. I could feel my dragon moving just beneath the surface. If I looked down, I was certain to see some scales covering my arm. He had already claimed her as his mate, but I would not unless she asked. At war with one's own beast was like being at war with yourself; split. Half of you wanted one thing so much it hurt, the other fought it with as much strength as possible.

"'Tis late, lad," my father's voice came from behind me. I had caught his scent earlier and turned to see him dressed in his furs, his thick white hair hanging down to below his shoulders, his brown eyes, knowing. "Are you well?"

"Aye," I answered. "Needed some fresh air."

"Ah," he replied in that all too knowing way of his. "How is our lass?"

"She sleeps," I stated, still staring out toward the ocean. The ledge was one of my favorite places. The back entrance to the keep with a stair to the king's chambers, provided an escape for the queen and the females, if there was an invasion.

"Something troubles you, lad," my father said.

"Aye," I answered.

"You may confide in me, if you so desire," he offered.

I was silent for a moment then looked down and spoke low.

"I am at war with my dragon. He wants to avenge her but the rational human side of me is telling him to wait. She begged me to be released and it made me feel as if I was keeping her prisoner. I want to do something for her, but it will go against your commands."

"What command and what do you desire to do?" he asked.

Turning to my father, I explained my idea.

Brigid

Something warm lay beside me. I was not sure what it was, but the moment a wet nose touched my arm, I shrieked and turned. Lir rose up beside me and pounced, licking my face.

"Lir?" I cried. The grey deerhound pulled back and looked at me, then licked my face again. "What are you doing here? How are you here?" I buried my face in the coarse fur of my deerhound and cried. His whimper caused me to pull away and look at him. He licked away my tears and I threw my arms around his neck crying harder.

Finn.

He was the only one who knew, and he had promised to do everything in his power to save him.

I had to find him. I needed to thank him. There was a knock at the door and Sara poked her head in, carrying a tray of food to break my fast.

"Och, what a beautiful beast!" she cried. Lir turned and barked a warning. Sara put her hands on her hips. "Och now we'll be having none of that, me wee beastie." Lir's tail began wagging faster and faster. "Better." Sara sat on my bed and petted Lir.

"Where is Finn?" I asked.

"He is still a bed," she replied. "But you cannae see him. 'Tis no' right. You are nae married yet. Twould be a scandal."

I did not say anything about how we spent the evening before in each other's company.

"Please, I must thank him," I stated.

She huffed. "I suppose, so long as you donnae tell anyone."

I nodded and stood. Grabbing the plaid from over the chair, I wrapped it around me and tiptoed to the door. Turning back to Sara I asked, "Which room is his?"

"Down the hall last door on the left," she answered.

"I thank you, truly," I replied and opened the door. Peering out, I felt Lir edge between my leg and the door frame squeezing his big body through the small opening.

"Mistress," the lass called. "Hurry back, and donnae let anyone see you."

"Aye, I promise I will return soon. Come Lir, find Finn." My pup put his nose to the ground and sniffed. We made our way quietly down the hall and once we came to the last door on the left, Lir scratched at the door and whimpered. "Shh, donnae wake the whole keep."

Just as I said that, the door opened, and I squealed. Finn stood there, a plaid wrapped around his hips, staring at me.

"Brigid?" he looked down the hallway. "What are you doing here?"

"I ken 'tis against tradition, but I had to see you," I said then looked down at Lir who was looking up at him and wagging his tail, banging it against the doorjamb.

"Och," he grinned and bent down, taking Lir's big head in his hands and scratching the pup behind the ears. "Did you wake your mistress, lad? We talked about this." Lir's tail wagged faster and he lunged forward to lick his face. "Och, you silly pup."

Tears gathered in my eyes as I watched my dragonman play with my pup. Finn looked up at me with a happy grin and a twinkle in his eye. My heart lurched and felt strangely light and heavy at the same time.

"You seemed so lonely without him last eve, lass," Finn said standing. "I wanted to have him here for you when you woke. I promised you, I would take care of him."

Without thought, I threw my arms around his neck and buried my face into his warm skin.

"Thank you," I said.

"Omph," he grunted and then held me close to him. He took a deep breath in, scenting my neck. Then, he pulled back. "You are very welcome. Now get you back to your chamber before someone sees you." He winked.

I nodded and kissed the spot that dipped just below his right ear, then turned to go. Lir's head whipped between the two of us. "Come, Lir." I called. He whimpered and sat down at Finn's feet. "Come now." He looked up at Finn, who laughed and motioned toward me.

"Go with your mistress," he ordered. "We will all be together soon." Lir's tail, even sitting, began to thump and then he stood and rushed down the hall to my room. With a final glance at Finn, he winked and disappeared back into his chamber.

Chapter Eleven

Finn

Her face was worth it all. After speaking with my father that evening, I had gained his permission to fly back to Lewis land and seek out Brigid's cottage. The pup barked at me from the ground as I circled. The dog was a fierce as his mistress. When I landed, I shifted back to my human form and took out a piece of Brigid's hair ribbon I had commandeered, before I had left her room. The dog cautiously came towards me as I beckoned. Once he could smell his mistress on the ribbon and he sniffed me, no doubt smelling her as well, he sat, allowing me to pet his head.

"Lir?" I questioned. He barked softly. "You need to come with me, lad, your mistress misses you." Again, he barked, stood and walked around in a circle. Looking up, I saw the cottage that had been Brigid's home for however long. Stepping closer to the door, I turned to look at the hound. He paced but did not stop me. Opening the door, I peeked in. The cottage was small, but it felt like her. Several herbs hung drying near the cold fireplace. I took a couple in my hand and smelled. Lavender, Rosemary, Tormentil, Bogweed. She had quite the collection. Unhooking the bundles, I put them in the small pouch I had tied to my ankle. I wasn't sure if she would need them, but the idea I could bring her something from her home was too much of a temptation. Once I looked around, I did not see anything else personal, my heart hurt for her. So lonely and with no one to protect her. Not that she truly needed it, I chuckled, my hand going to the non-existent scar on my chest. That was going to change. I would always protect her. We would be partners.

Walking back out of the cottage, I looked toward Lir who was watching me with his head cocked to one side.

"I need you to trust me, lad," I said. Lir stood on all fours and sniffed me once more. I beckoned to the carrier I had brought with me. Tossing Brigid's hair ribbon into the carrier, I coaxed the pup to enter. The walls were high enough he could not jump out, but it included the added benefit of having a buckle at the top making sure to keep whatever was in the carrier secure. Lir did not give me much fuss and as I flew back to my father's lands, the pup slept.

I landed at the west entrance ledge, the same place I spoke with my father. Gently setting the carrier down, I shifted and accepted the plaid from my father, who was waiting for me. Unbuckling the top, I lowered the side and coaxed the pup out.

"Och, what a beautiful creature," my father praised. "You must be hungry, lad." As Lir's tail began to wag, my father chuckled. "I will take care of the pup. Your mother and sister just landed. They wish to see you." My face must have betrayed my thoughts for my father continued. "I will not steal your lass's appreciation, lad. I will merely get this handsome devil some water and a leg of mutton. Go to your mother. I will join you as soon as he eats.

I nodded and thanked him. Hurrying to the trunk against the wall, I pulled out one of the clean tunics we kept for situations such as this. Once dress, I took the back stairs two at a time and reached my mother's solar.

"Come in," I heard after I knocked. Opening the door, my youngest sibling squealed and rushed into my arms.

"Och, Tahra," I held my sister close. "You have grown! Are you certain you were only gone for a month?"

She giggled and held on me.

"I am nineteen, most dragonwomen of my age grow quickly," she replied.

"Aye," I pulled back and observed her. "I will need to be sure you are kept far away from the dragonmen," I teased. She blushed and looked down.

"That is precisely what your grandfather said," my mother answered, walking over to me.

"I guarantee he did," I smiled and embraced her.

"How are you, my dear one?" she asked. "I have heard of some of your experiences from your father. Come in and tell us about the lass you are to mate the day after tomorrow."

I nodded and allowed my mother and sister to pull me further into the room, to a chair by the fire.

"She is..." I sighed thanking my sister for a glass of spiced wine. "I donnae know what to say. She is an extraordinary human. I know you will love her."

"What is her name?" Tahra asked.

"Brigid," I answered. "She is of marrying age, a healer, and a warrior."

"And do you like her?" my mother asked.

"Aye, I do," I answered. "I do like her."

"But you donnae *love* her," Tahra stated.

"I hardly know her, little sister," I replied. "Love can come in time."

"Indeed, look at your father and I," my mother said.

"What about you and me, love?" my father's voice came from the doorway. My mother grinned seeing her husband and rose to greet him.

"Och, what a beautiful wee pup!" Tahra cried and knelt to greet the grey dog who bounded over to her and licked her outstretched hand. Lir was hardly small, but to dragons he was... wee.

"'Tis Brigid's," my father said, holding his wife to his side. "Finn went this very night to retrieve him."

"What is his name?" Tahra asked playing with him.

"Lir," I said. "But I do need to take him to her chamber. I want her to wake to him."

"You are a romantic, like your father," my mother teased.

"It won your favor, did it not?" my father asked.

"Many times. Why do you think we have so many whelps?" my mother replied.

"Because you cannae keep your hands to yourself, wife" Da' teased and leaned down to kiss her.

"Tahra," I called well aware of where their banter was headed. "Perhaps we should leave our parents to their... conversation."

"'Tis not what they call it these days, lad," my father laughed.

"Tender ears," Ma slapped his chest in reproach.

"Och, mate, you had better hold off on doing that until we are alone." His eyes flashed to his dragon slits and my mother laughed.

"Easy, dragonman. I ken you missed me, but patience is a virtue." Da' claimed her lips and Tahra and I gathered our things.

"Come, sister," I said. "Come now, Lir," the dog whipped

his head around at the sound of his name and trotted alongside Tahra and out the door. "Good evening," I called to my parents but was not surprised to not receive an answer. Tahra and I walked together down the stairs from the solar and down the corridor to her room.

"I find it sweet our parents still love each other after all this time," Tahra said. "I hope and pray for a love like theirs."

"We both do, dear one. But since when are you considering marriage?" I asked. She looked away. "Has someone caught your eye?"

"Nay," she hastily said. "At least, not one who would consider me."

"And who would *not* consider you? You are daughter to the king," I wrapped an arm around her shoulders in comfort.

"And the youngest of *four* brothers..." she reminded me.

"Och aye, but it is a brother's prerogative to tease his sister's mate. Keeps the dragon inline. No one unworthy will have my sister."

"Aye," she sighed. "I know it well."

I let it drop for the time, as we walked together. I saw my sister safely to her chamber and then walked quietly with Lir by my side, to Brigid's room. Lir whined and scratched at the door when he smelled his mistress's scent.

"Easy lad, donnae wake her," I whispered. Lir looked up at me and almost as if he understood, he bowed his head. "Good, lad. Now go," I whispered and opened the door just a crack. Lir squeezed in and followed her scent to the bed. My dragon fire was still burning in the hearth and I saw Brigid asleep on the bed. Resting on her side, the furs were bunched up under her arm as if she held something to her. She was curled up close to the edge and looked so small. My chest ached as I watched Lir jump on the bed, circle around, and lay beside her. I wanted to be the one to lay beside her. I wanted to hold her, protect her. My thoughts worried me. It was unlike me to feel that way.

When a dragon claims his mate, he falls quickly and hard. My feelings worried me as did my dragon's possessiveness of her. I had to keep my distance if I had any chance of surviving when she left.

Shaking my head, I stopped my thoughts. She was not mine, nor would she be. We would share a chamber, aye, but that was as far as it could go. I needed to look at her differently and stop allowing her sweet nature, fiery passion, and soft lips distract me. I had a duty to the clan to mate and reproduce, but it would not be with her. Lir lifted his grey head as I closed the door. Lifting a finger to my lips, I told the pup to be quiet and closed the door behind me.

Making my way down the hall to my own chamber, I noticed the pale light of predawn begin to light the sky. I needed sleep and quickly if I was not to fall asleep at my own prewedding dinner tomorrow. I hoped our discussion would prepare her for what would happen. With that in mind, I stripped out of my clothes and fell into my bed, pulling the furs up to my waist. I closed my eyes and calmed my inner dragon. Peace. Sleep. But the lass's blue eyes haunted me, and I found little sleep that night.

Chapter Twelve

Erina, Queen of the Dragons

"You are keeping secrets from me," I said as my husband and I lay together in our bed. He slowly stroked my back with his fingertips. I snuggled deeper into him. Nearly thirty years of marriage and Edan still made me feel loved, cherished, and desired. I also very much enjoyed his *welcome home.*

"Secrets? Me?" he asked, kissing my hair.

"Aye, you, oh great king of dragons," I leaned up on my elbow and laughed when his eyes dropped to my bare chest. "You are insatiable. Even after twice, you still want more."

Gripping me to him, he kissed me again. "Aye, but I only feel this way for you, my love."

"Because you know that if it is for anyone but me, I would take your manhood," I grinned.

"Och, aye, I know that," he answered.

"But you are keeping secrets from me." Finn's face flashed in my mind. Something wasn't right. A mother always knew when something was wrong with her child and my dragon sensed his unease.

"What secrets would that be?" He asked coyly.

"About Finn," I answered. "Tell me truthfully, love. Does he not want to marry the lass?"

"'Tis a long conversation, but I do have his permission to speak to you. I would not betray his confidence otherwise."

"I know you would not," I said. "But as his mother, I need to know he is safe."

"Then, my love, let me tell you what a great male your son is," my mate turned on his side and began the story.

Brigid

With Lir at my side, I ate breakfast in my chamber and then sought Finn. One of the guards told me he was with his father in the king's solar and escorted me to the door. Knocking, I heard Edan call for me to enter.

"Forgive me for interrupting," I curtsied to the king when I caught his eyes. Finn stood to his father's right.

"Nae interruption," the king smiled warmly at me. "What can we do for you, lass?"

"I was hoping, if it was permitted, to go for a walk outside. I promise to nae move further than the bailey."

"Ah, of course," the king agreed. "The weather is fair. It is a beautiful day. Finn?"

"Of course, Brigid, you are no' a prisoner here. You are free to roam as you see fit. I only ask, as one befitting your station, you take two guards with you."

"If that is the condition, I would be happy to."

"Good," Finn called for two of the men standing outside the door. "You will accompany Mistress Lewis wherever she may desire to go." They said nothing only bowed to their prince.

"I thank you for your protection," I said to the guards then turned back to Finn. "Thank you."

Finn bowed slightly to me. I turned to leave when the king called me back. "Lass," he said. "My wife and daughter have arrived and would love to meet you. Donnae be a stranger if you see them."

"Of course, I would love to meet her majesty. How will I know her?" I asked.

"Och, by her beauty. There is no lass who compares to her," the king sighed.

I nodded, though I was no closer knowing what the queen looked like.

"She has my color hair, stands to my father's brow and has my eyes, Brigid," Finn explained.

Smiling, I thanked him, and the two men followed me as I bowed and left the room.

Walking through the bailey, seeing the clan going about their day, gave me a chance to reconsider everything I had been taught. I always swore I would never judge too quickly; it was a good trait for a healer to have. But walking outside in the bailey, seeing the keep come alive as any other, I realized how quick I was to judge this land and these people... dragons. They were no different than the Lewis clan nor the other clans I had visited to tend the sick. They worked the lands, raised their young, cooked, celebrated, and mourned. The fact they could change into dragons and breathe fire, was nearly a moot point. Nearly.

Feeling the two guards walking slowly and at a safe distance behind me, I came to a wall of tan colored stone cut into the mountain. My fingers touched the stone, marveling at the master masonry needed to build such a large and intricate building.

"Beautiful, isn't it, my lady?" I heard a voice from behind me say. Turning, I noticed the guards had turned to face each other, their gazes and stances at attention. Kai, Finn's dearest friend, stood before me.

"It is, indeed, Master Kai," I admitted. Not knowing his true rank, though knowing he must be of some status for Finn to be friends with him and the guards' reactions, I curtsied. My uncle never spoke to someone if they were beneath him in rank.

"I am War Chief, lass," he explained almost as if he could read my mind.

"Apologies, Chief MacKay," I corrected, giving him the honor due one so powerful within the clan and in the laird's confidence.

"Nae need for that," he waved me off. "Only to merely introduce myself to ye properly."

"It is an honor, Chief," I replied. "You will remain in the position under Finn, correct?"

"Aye, I will. Unless challenged."

"Is that likely?" I asked.

"Nay," he replied. "But a good warrior prepares for every eventuality."

We were quiet for a long moment, but I sensed there was more he wanted to say.

"Speak freely, Chief MacKay," I offered. "I am new here and hope we can become friends. I ask you to speak your mind."

Glancing at his men, he spoke. "Leave us for a moment." They said nothing only bowed and walked a short distance away. Kai stared at me for a while, then huffed a sigh.

"There is a rumor going around that you are nae willing to join with our prince in marriage. A rumor that you were not given a choice."

"You donnae strike me as a man who listens to gossip."

"Normally no, but if that is true," he held up his hand, preventing me from saying anything. "Please, I care not in so far as the future of the clan and my best friend's happiness. If that is true, I beg you, say nothing. Finn is an honorable male and one who deserves to be king. His brothers are only too eager to use anything they can against him. I implore you... be as a wife to him. Show the clan they have nothing to fear."

I was quiet for a long moment. How could I do as he asked? *Could I?*

"Though I take your advice as a friend, Chief MacKay, I will have you understand one thing. My desire is to assist Finn not tear him down. He is to be my husband, king, and laird. I would ask you, who spread these rumors?" I demanded. He stared at me again but this time, telling me all I needed to know. "Cahal." I breathed. Kai nodded. "I thank you for your candor, Chief MacKay," I stated. "And I will consider your advice."

He bowed and without another word, he marched back to the bailey giving me a chance to think.

My deerhound lay near the hearth of my room, Finn's white dragon fire was still lit. Sara pulled out a new gown for me to wear to dinner. She had assisted me with a bath and had plaited my long red hair in a fashion that I had to admit was beautiful. I never liked my hair, it was unruly and stubborn, but as I sat looking at the ringlets framing my face, cascading down my back, my heart was in my throat.

How could I go through with this on the current terms with Finn? My eyes turned to Lir laying nearby, his eyebrows moving back and forth as he looked up at Sara and me. Finn would make no designs on me. I kept repeating. I had no choice but to make the bargain. I could not love him. I could not be his wife in truth. I did not know him. As sweet as he was, I did not want to be in a loveless marriage. There was no choice for many lasses, but I always wanted what my parents had. A true love.

A knock at the door had me looking up and even Lir raised his head. One of the most beautiful women I had ever seen, poked her head in and smiled. Sara curtsied, causing me to stand.

"Och, you must be Brigid," the woman said, and I distinctly heard an Irish accent. I curtsied.

"Aye, your majesty," I replied, realizing she must be the queen and Finn's mother. The eyes and the shape of the mouth were the same.

"Oh, no need for that," she answered, then turned to Sara. "Please give us a moment?" Sara curtsied again and left the room, shutting the door behind her. My palms suddenly grew sweaty under the gaze of this dragon woman. Her brown hair was plaited in braids and her gown was a deep burgundy. "My son is a treasure, is he not?" She asked, walking over to Lir who stood, tail wagging allowing the queen to pet him.

"Aye, your majesty. He is a wonderful man."

"My name is Erina, dear," she smiled softly. Lowering her voice, she continued. "My husband has told me of your arrangement. I am so sorry you were treated so unfairly by your clan. I hope you can consider us your new family. We will care for you."

"I thank you, Erina," I said.

"He also told me of your *other* arrangement," she stated. I looked down and twisted my fingers. "Forgive me, but as a female, I want you to know, I understand completely." I looked up sharply.

"You do?" I asked.

"Aye," she answered. "You see, my husband and I did not know each other until a week before our wedding. For some, that is enough. For others, a lifetime isn't enough to fall in love. The first moment I saw Edan, I thought there was no possibility of me falling in love with him. He was pompous, arrogant, and chased any female who looked at him. I refused him on our wedding night. I told him he would have to prove himself to me before I took him to my bed. When he realized I was serious, a change came over him. Never have I seen a man attempt to reign in his dragon so strongly. Over the next several months I found myself falling deeper and deeper in love with him. It was the little things. Bringing me a certain flower I loved or ordering a dish I had mentioned I enjoyed. He did things to make me see he cared.

"One night, I went to his chamber and told him how I felt. He then told me, he had been in love with me since he first saw me, in my dragon form. My human form was just an added benefit. I knew then I would accept him, if he asked. And when he did, we consummated our marriage. Never have I been happier and that dragonman has proven to me every day I made the right choice. I tell you this, not to tell you intimate details about the king and myself, but to tell you, I commend you for your fortitude. But I will tell you, my son is a wonderful male and any woman would be fortunate to have him as a husband."

"I am grateful for your counsel, your majesty... Erina," I said. "But it is not only that... I lost my mother at a very young age."

"Ah," Erina nodded. "Lass, I am sorry for your loss."

"I thank you, but though I am a healer and have been told what happens between a husband and wife, I have never had a *mother's* counsel for such matters," I replied.

"Oh, I see," Erina said. "I would be happy to counsel you in this if you desire it, at any time."

"Finn has told me he will not request that of me," I explained.

"Aye," Erina answered. "But perhaps you will one day desire to be married in truth, to my son or not. I would be happy to speak with you, as a mother."

"I thank you," I looked down. Even after telling this

woman I would not be a true wife to her son, she still wished to help me.

"Now, I ken this is only your second dinner, but it is slightly different than the first night. There is no need for a kiss to please the clan, but if you need either Finn or myself do not hesitate to ask."

"Truly, I thank you for your hospitality," I said.

"We are a clan, lass," she replied. Then walking over to the chair beside the fire, she took the sash with such reverence and walked towards me. "You wear the colors of our clan, Brigid. May I have the honor of placing this around you?"

I nodded and Erina wrapped the plaid sash around me, pinning it with the clan's brooch at my hip. The weight and meaning behind what she just did made me shudder. Erina took my shoulders in her hands and made me look at her.

"You are a part of our clan now and forever. And we protect what is ours. Allow Finn to be your protector, your champion. I ask one thing from you, lass."

"Aye, my lady?"

"Do not embarrass my son before his clan," she said. "He is to be king and if the clan thinks he is too weak to bed his wife, they will never follow him. If he needs you to be there as if a lover, be there for him, even though you will never carry his young. If a time comes when he is victorious in battle or in sparring before he releases you, I ask you do as a wife and welcome him home properly for all the clan to see." I took a deep breath before answering.

"I would never want to embarrass Finn, my queen," I said. "I swear to you on all I hold dear, my last wish would be to cause him to look weak in the eyes of his clan. I do care for him. And I thank him for his consideration. Not many men would offer what he offered. If the time comes as you say, I will welcome him home as my husband and a woman trying to be worthy of his love."

"You are more than worthy of his love," she answered. "And I am pleased to see the truth in your eyes. Forgive a mother's overprotective nature toward her eldest. Know that so long as I live, you will have my protection as a mother."

"I do miss my mother and I thank you for your offer," I said.

Erina nodded and kissed my forehead. "Now, we must go to dinner. Come."

I thanked her once and we headed out the door and down the hall.

Chapter Thirteen

Finn

Sitting with my father and brothers waiting for my bride, mother, and sister to appear, I forced the bouncing of my knee to stop as I gripped my mug of ale a wee bit too hard. She had all day to herself to walk around the grounds and though my men kept me appraised of where she was at all times, they could not tell me anything regarding her mood or apparent enjoyment of what she saw. Did she like the isles? Did she want to return to Lewis lands? Did anyone frighten her? In conference with my father and his council for most of the day, I had no time to check in with her before I needed to prepare for supper. But now, waiting far longer than should be, I cursed the time away from her.

"Dear me, Da', I do believe Finn is anxious to see his intended bride," Bearcbhan's voice came from beside Teyrnon.

"Donnae tease your brother, Bearcbhan," Da' said next.

"He is just as anxious as you were, if you recall."

"Aye, well, at least with mine we kenned each other a lot longer. Our wedding night was... quite enjoyable."

Cahal attempted to stand, but father's hand on his arm stopped him. I refused to dignify Bearcbhan's taunt but did feel a pang of pity for my brother. Cahal never was the same after Bearcbhan and Sybine mated.

"I am sure my wedding night will be just as satisfying, Bearcbhan. Besides as your elder brother I am much more adapt to wooing pretty lasses and knowing my place when it comes to finding them." That shut him up quickly.

Looking down, Bearcbhan found the tails of his tunic fascinating. Cahal looked over at me and I tried to smile at him. He nodded his thanks. That was progress, I supposed. Cahal and I used to be best friends, the closest in age, we grew up together. But five years ago, he changed. His dragon going nearly rogue. I normally never got involved in whatever was between Cahal and Bearcbhan but enough was enough. I could take taunting me, but when Bearcbhan deliberately tried to wound Cahal by throwing barbs, I refused to let it go unanswered. Since my father was stepping down in eight months, wrangling my brothers would become my duty and the gods help me, it will leave little time for much else.

"Where are they, dammit?" Teyrnon demanded, uncharacteristically. "We cannae eat until they arrive, and I am famished."

"They will be here when they are ready," Da' said.

"Do you think something is wrong?" Bearcbhan asked his eyes drifting to the stairs.

"Nay," Da' replied. "I believe your mother may have met Brigid in her chamber and they are speaking."

"Should I go and make sure they are well?" I offered.

"No need," Da' said standing, eyes on the stairs. Instinctually, we all stood too. "They are here."

My eyes trailed to the four women stepping down from the stone stairs. My mother unescorted, as was usual for the queen, stepped forward and locked eyes with my father. The queen was not to be escorted by any save the king. Her guards came up behind her, moving from their position flanking the stair. Sybine was next, escorted by one of the men assigned to her as protection. She looked up and smiled at her husband. Brigid was behind her, also unescorted like my mother. And my sister Tahra was the last.

Brigid's beauty drew my attention and seeing my clan colors around her shoulders, took my breath. But soon a cold chill snaked its way down my back as I saw Kai, my best friend and War Chief move from his place at the foot of the stairs to beside my sister. Kissing her hand, he bowed to her then he moved to my future bride. Kai should never escort either of them. When Brigid looked at him confused my dragon calmed. Kai smiled at her, leaned in, and whispered something to her, then bowed and walked back to my sister.

My dragon growled. He was not worthy of such a position and as both were unattached, gossip would spread. Only when I saw the look in Tahra's eyes as she looked up at him did I nearly walk over. My father's hand on my arm held me back.

"Do not make a scene," he whispered harshly.

"He is not worthy of her. I must put a stop to this."

"We will do no such thing," Da' ordered. "He is War Chief and therefore, very worthy."

"But, Da'," I reasoned, his eyes flashed to dragon slits then back to his human. I lowered my eyes. He was still my king and I should never question him before others. My brothers were watching us.

"We will discuss this later."

Even nearing thirty, when my father spoke those words, my palms grew sweaty and my heart pounded like I was a boy again. He was not happy with me.

"Forgive me," I whispered. "I respect your decision."

"Do not forget whose child she is, Finn. She is your *sister*, not your *daughter*. You have no right to choose for her."

"Are you truly encouraging such a union?" I questioned. But of course, Da' did not know. Kai and I would go to the local human village, before I knew I was to marry Brigid. They had a tavern and most of the women there knew us by name and some kenned us intimately. Da' did not know Kai's... inclinations. One woman was never enough and at times he liked to keep them tied up. The first time I saw it, I nearly challenged him, but he claimed the woman enjoyed it. I would not see my sister with a rogue like that. He was my best friend, aye, but he was not for Tahra. Shaking the disturbing image that made its way into my head, I turned back to my father. "I would speak with you about him before you make a choice, if agreeable."

"Later," my father said as our women arrived at the dais.

My father and brother met their wives with a kiss and a twinkle in their eyes, one my siblings and I long ago figured meant more than we ever desired to know. Sybine took Bearcbhan's hand and they kissed gently. No doubt Bearcbhan was worried about my reaction.

Offering my hand to Brigid, her slim fingers slipped into mine. Loving the feel of her softly calloused skin, I raised her hand to my lips and kissed her knuckles. Her blush gave me a moment's pause but soon the king bellowed to begin the feast. Brigid allowed me to lead her to the table and sat between my mother and me. She was quiet, almost timid. My warrior maiden had something on her mind.

Catching Tahra's eye, I smiled at her and took Brigid's hand again. She turned to me.

"Allow me, Brigid to introduce my sister, Tahra," I indicated her across the way from my mother. "Tahra, my future bride, Brigid Lewis."

"I am so pleased to meet you properly, Brigid. I hope we will be great friends," Tahra said eagerly.

Brigid smiled at her. "A pleasure, Tahra and aye I am sure we will be."

My sister merely smiled widely and turned her attention back to our father. Brigid leaned into me and I lowered my ear to her.

"We met in the hallway upstairs, but it was good to meet her properly. How old is she?" she whispered.

"Nineteen," I answered. "She and my mother go every year to visit my grandfather and uncles and aunts in Ireland. I believe my uncle, the king, is trying to arrange a marriage with her. He has only sons and no one to join the clans."

"Does she know this is a possibility?"

"I am sure she does, but she has said nothing to me. It is merely a feeling. Da' would never allow it."

"Do you not think it would be prudent to speak to her about it?"

"Why worry her? It will come to naught."

"Perhaps, but I know I would rather know."

I took a deep breath and nodded slowly. She, of course spoke from experience.

"Well, it will be nice to get to know her… for however long I will be here with you," she looked down and for a moment, I wondered, what was on her mind.

"Aye, I am glad you will have a friend, lass, but there are two others I would like you to meet after dinner."

"Oh? Of course."

"Good, now enjoy. I donnae believe you will find finer meat nor better wine apart from the wedding feast itself."

She took a bite of the meat and closed her eyes. I was not lying when I bragged about the taste. Dragons slow roasted the boar on a spit outside the bailey using dragon fire. The high heat along with some herbs and spices rubbed on the outside trapped in the flavors and juices and then it slowly roasted over a much lower flame. The flavors burst over the tongue with earthly, rosemary and sage. Brigid looked over at me and wiped her mouth after she swallowed.

"That was beyond delicious," she agreed. "Is that not common fare?"

"We usually have something similar, but they prepare the best for holidays and weddings," I explained.

"I will miss this until there is another celebration."

My heart fluttered for a moment at her words. Then, as if she realized what she said, she cleared her throat gently and looked down.

"I will be sure to have them make this again for you before..." I couldn't bring myself to say *before you leave me* and from the look in her eyes, she couldn't either.

"I thank you for caring," she said.

"Of course, lass," I replied. I debated but kenned Brigid would understand. "Could I beg a womanly confidence of you, lass?" She nodded. "Did my sister say anything about Kai?"

Brigid blushed and my hand clenched. Did *she* want Kai?

"I can only tell you what I saw," she began. "They met at the top of the stairs and she seemed excited to see him, but she knew her place as princess and waited until he greeted her properly. He asked your mother's permission to escort her. Truly, I was surprised when he came to me, I was told it was not done but he whispered something to me."

"Can you tell me what he said? I will see him punished if he made you uncomfortable." She looked up at me, horror in her eyes. "Even if he is my friend, your safety is paramount to me, lass."

Her eyes drifted to the gathered dragons. My gaze followed her to see Kai, seated with others of his warriors, watching us. I looked back at Brigid, but she would not raise her eyes to mine. A pang of jealously rushed through me and my dragon's nostrils curled smoke. So, my best friend *was* after my female. Before I realized it, I stood with the express purpose of challenging him, when Brigid placed a hand on my arm.

"Please," she pleaded. "He only asked me to not embarrass you. He meant nae disrespect." Her words somehow registered and I sat back down.

"Did he speak with you?" I demanded.

"Aye, earlier today. You are fortunate to have such a loyal friend and War Chief. He wanted to say his piece and he did so respectfully. Apparently, there's a rumor going around that I am no' a willing bride."

"Who started such a rumor?" I breathed, sitting back down. Her eyes drifted to Cahal, not watching anything, merely eating the rest of his food, eyes on his plate.

"It matters not, but we must be cautious. I would never desire to give them any chance or fodder to dethrone you."

What a queen she would make. But I felt immediately guilty for believing the worst of Kai. I decided to say no more and soon we turned back to our meal and my father's story. Everything newly discovered still churned in my mind.

Chapter Fourteen

Brigid

Sitting beside Finn, I leaned back allowing the serving women to clear my place. I watched the main dining hall. Eyes glanced our way, but I saw only curiosity and interest, no hostility or distrust. Finn's concern for his sister and his worry over me, was endearing, but I also worried. He seemed to be becoming far too attached to me and I had no wish to hurt him when I left. I tasted the bile on my tongue as I thought of leaving. What other choice did I have? I could not stay... *could I?* My eyes drifted toward the tables and the clan who so quickly took me as one of their own. I could find happiness and peace here.

I caught two women standing from their tables beside two men and heading our way.

"Finn?" I questioned softly not wanting to interrupt Erina as she spoke to the table. Finn glanced at me and leaned down when I motioned for him. Whispering, I continued. "Who are those women?" They walked up to the steps of the dais. He looked over and smiled. They waited patiently at the foot of the stairs.

Erina ended her story and Finn motioned for the attention. "Forgive me, but I have asked Cara and Ailidh to speak with Brigid. I will just see to their comfort by the fire and will return."

"Oh, of course, darling. Wonderful idea," Erina said. "In fact, it is well past the time Tahra and I retire. We will see you tomorrow." Erina and her daughter stood. I had very little time to meet Tahra but from the short conversation I had with her, the nineteen-year-old struck me very much like her brother Finn. They even had the same smile. Tahra said good night to her brothers and received a kiss on her cheek from each of them and her father. Passing me, she took my hand and smiled.

"I am glad to have met you, Brigid," she said. "I am sure we will be friends."

"I would like that," I replied. Erina embraced me quickly and they both left the room.

"I will get you settled before the fireplace, Brigid. But if you need me, I will be here with my brothers and father," Finn offered his hand to me.

"Of course, but who are they?"

"They are two of the other human lasses married into our clan from the Lewis. As you ken, every twenty years was the treaty. Ailidh has been with our clan for forty years and Cara twenty."

I nodded. It was almost too much to hope for other humans to be part of the clan even though Finn had told me the terms. I looked over at the two women and smiled. I was not alone in a clan filled with dragons.

"Would you like to speak with them, lass?" Finn asked.

"Very much," I replied. The younger one, Cara, I seemed to remember meeting before, but it was only flashes.

Finn offered his hand to me and escorted me to the fireplace, the two women following close behind. Once we were situated, Finn made the introductions.

"It is a pleasure to meet you, my lady," Cara, the younger woman said. "I remember you as a young girl."

"And I you," I replied. "Though it is only flashes. I am sorry."

"Oh, donnae apologize, my lady," she said. "You were but three at most. I visited with my husband many times. My sister and nephew still live amongst the Lewis."

"You have the true look of your mother, sweet lady," the older lady, Ailidh said.

"You knew my mother?" I sat up.

"Indeed," she replied. "We both did. She was younger than me, but I remember her well, and your father."

Tears gathered in my eyes and I felt Finn's hand squeeze mine.

"Oh, my lady, I did nae mean to cause you pain," she hurried to say.

"Nay," I assured. "It has been so long since anyone spoke to me freely of them, I find I was overcome with happiness and yet sadness."

"I heard they died," Cara softly comforted. "I am sorry."

"As am I, lass," Ailidh said. "I too, lost my mother at a young age. I share your pain."

"Thank you, but I did nae loose her. She was taken from me. Stolen. Murdered," the vehemence in my tone surprised even me.

The two women glanced at Finn who leaned over to me and whispered softly, "vengeance will be had on them, mark my words, lass."

I nodded, pleased to hear his promise. I was never blood

thirsty, but I could not bring myself to care how it looked.

"Now, though, I shall leave you, if you so desire," Finn continued. "Cara and Ailidh have been gracious enough to offer their knowledge and support as you adjust to your new life... here." *For as long as you are here*, was left unsaid but Finn squeezed my hand, stood, nodded to both women, and left the area. My gaze followed him, not knowing the women watched me and waited for my permission to sit. Finally, when one of them giggled. I looked at them, a blush coloring my cheeks.

"Forgive me."

"Nay nay," they both waved me off.

"I believe we both remember the feeling," Cara stated.

"Please sit," I offered seeing Ailidh nod in agreement.

Both women sat beside me, our chairs situated so we could lean together and have an intimate conversation or pull back and watch the music and dancing on the main level.

"I remember my second night here, my lady. It was so different from what I knew but I will tell you, there is no clan tighter woven or stronger than the MacKays. And no males more loving, passionate and protective as the dragonmen," Ailidh said.

"It can be overwhelming at first but soon you come to know they would do anything for you, and it is a form of love, you never tire of," Cara offered.

"Did you know the clan before you married?" I asked careful not to ask my burning question of; *did you know dragons were real before one picked you up off the ground?*

"Aye, in so far as the treaty and what is expected of me," Cara offered.

"In my time," Ailidh began. "Dragons traded with us openly. I recall seeing many in flight over my family's farm as a young lass. I always wondered how the ground looked from up there. But that was under your grandfather's rule..."

"My uncle put a stop to it?"

"Almost immediately, your grandfather not cold in his grave."

"Why?"

"He never gave a reason."

I paused wondering if Edan kenned why. I wanted to ask but turned back to the ladies. "Did you both know your husbands before you were chosen?" I asked.

They both shook their heads.

"I met Odalis two nights before our mating ceremony," Cara's eyes scanned the gathered clansmen and fell on one man in particular. He was handsome, his slightly advanced years gave him an appeal. His grey and brown hair hung to his shoulders, his dancing dark eyes caught hers and a smirk lifted the side of his lip as he winked at her. Gazing back to Cara, I saw a blush tinge her cheeks, but she winked back then looked down and cleared her throat when Ailidh laughed.

"Aye, aye our dragon men are a randy lot," Ailidh stated. "But there is no greater loving than that given by your dragon. It is true what they say, dragons are kenned far and wide for their... well-deserved lovemaking skills."

I felt a deep blush color my cheeks. I could never tell these women that my dragonman would never be able to show me his skills.

"Now, ask us anything, my lady. Anything at all. We will nae gossip and nothing after forty years can embarrass me," Ailidh said.

"Nor me," Cara replied. "We are your personal confidants, my lady."

"Please call me Brigid," I said. "I donnae ken if I will ever be used to *my lady*."

"You will in time, Brigid. I am certain. Even *your majesty* will become second nature," Ailidh stated.

I was not sure how I felt about Ailidh's words and nature. Part of me loved that she held nothing back and spoke her mind, but part of me was not familiar enough with speaking to others to appreciate her bluntness at times.

"Do you have any concerns regarding the marriage bed with a dragonman?" Ailidh asked. I nearly choked and grabbed my spiced wine.

"Ehm, nay," I said. "That is..."

"'Tis all right, lass," she waved me off. "I ken how speaking to an old woman about that can be for one so young."

"I do believe it may be your manner, dear Ailidh," Cara smiled at the older woman.

"Och, I do apologize," Ailidh turned back to me with a hand over her heart, mortified. "Having lived with dragons for over forty years, I sometimes forget how humans take things."

"Nay, 'tis all right," I assured. "I am not used to speaking with people, let alone being direct. Please donnae worry. I know what to expect..." Then seeing their surprised faces, I clarified before they thought me a wanton. "That is, I have been told. I am a healer like my mother, so male form and the act is not foreign to me, in so far as a healer's knowledge." It was easier than confessing Finn would never be my husband in truth.

"Ah, of course. That is good then," Cara ended the questioning. Even when it looked like Ailidh would protest, Cara jumped in again. "Tell us, my lady, will you continue your healing practices here?"

"I am unsure what my duties will be, but I hope to."

"You are very much like your mother," Cara said. "She was always so thoughtful of others. I see her spark in your eyes."

"It is good to hear someone speak kindly about her since my..."

"Since what, my dear?" Ailidh asked.

"Well... my uncle called her a witch and had her burned.

Since then, no one spoke of her with kindness."

Cara and Ailidh gasped, their hands flying in unison to their chests. They said nothing but as fast as I could blink, Finn was by my side.

"Is all well?" he demanded.

"Aye," I replied, grateful for his comfort. "I merely told Cara and Ailidh my mother's fate, since they knew her."

"Och, lass, I am so sorry," Ailidh said, tears gathering in her eyes. "How terrible for you."

"It was and I lived in fear every day the same fate would befall me. But my uncle had his own thoughts. Perhaps he thought to sacrifice me to a dragon and that dragon would do it for him." A growl echoed in Finn's chest and I went on. "But little did he know, my dragonman is the very best of men."

Finn went still beside me. Why I was saying those things, I was unsure, but they were true. My uncle probably thought to give me to a dragon so I would meet my mother's fate. He did not know the dragons are kinder, gentler, and better men than he ever could be. Finn's and Edan's welcome had given me a sense of belonging and I was not willing to give it up. I shocked myself by thinking that. Could I want to stay... but not be married...yet?

Finn crouched down beside me and stared into my eyes. "Are you tired, lass?" he asked. "You have had a long day. I will escort you to your room, if you desire."

"Aye, thank you. I have much to prepare," I agreed. Turning back to the women, I smiled. "Thank you for your conversation, concern, and listening ear. I pray our friendship grows."

"As do we, my lady," Cara said. "If you have any questions or concerns, please do not hesitate to reach out. And allow your dragonman to take care of you. Believe me, though you can take care of yourself, there is nothing quite like it," she winked. After saying goodnight, we all stood. Finn offered his arm to me and I watched Cara and Ailidh walk to their husbands to be greeted with a passionate kiss and a promising wink.

I turned to look at Finn and studied him. His eyes were shuttered as if he did not want me to see too much of him. But the longer I stared the more I saw and the more I wondered, could the gods have smiled on me and could he be my fate?

Chapter Fifteen

Finn

The day had finally come. The day I would take Brigid as my mate. I stood at the front of the long walkway of the cave, my clan with me. My father stood to my side. The drummers were playing a rhythmic beat as the dragons danced around a fire my dragon had lit. To the outside world it would look pagan, but to us it was tradition and we were not worshiping anything but the gods that put us here. My brothers stood to my left, lining the cave wall.

"You have done a great thing, lad," my father said. "I am proud of you."

"I have had a good teacher, Da'," I answered. "I will strive every day to be as good a leader as you."

"Och, nay, be your own and be a better one than I," he said.

"That will be hard to accomplish," I replied.

"Good," he teased. Chuckling, my eyes were drawn to the front as the drummers dramatically stopped playing. Brigid and my mother stood at the entrance. Her white gown with my clan colors draped over her shoulder, made my dragon take notice. Her red hair was partially up with the remainder tumbling down her back. She wore no jewels as that was part of my gifts to her. Her eyes locked on mine and our clan chanter began with our clan moto deep and rumbling in his chest. Then the drummers began actively banging and the piper joined. My mother coaxed Brigid forward and her eyes left mine to look around the cave.

Soaring through the mountain, the room was large enough for twenty dragons to shift and fly. The chorus of voices joined in and Brigid's eyes flashed from one side to the other. The shadows of the dragon dancers flickered on the wall as she walked down the aisle towards me. My mother stayed back and just as I saw the fear in her eyes, Brigid looked at me. I pulled myself up and held her gaze. She blinked a few times and kept walking. Never breaking eye contact with me, she reached the steps and stayed two steps below my father and me. All at once the music stopped. A hush descended on the gathered and my father began.

"Brigid Lewis," his voice boomed. "You have come here to be attached to our clan through marriage. You have accepted my son Aodhfionn as your mate and husband. If you have any legitimate reason not to join with him, I ask you speak now, or never again."

She locked eyes with me, but I let it be her decision. If she chose to answer with aye, then she would be free. I would be looked upon as a bride thief, and it would give my brothers the perfect opportunity to challenge me for my first-born rights. If she chose nay, then our deal would continue. She pulled her eyes away from me and answered my father.

"Nay, I have no legitimate reason not to join with him," she answered.

My father nodded once and looked over at me.

"Aodhfionn," he began. "Step down and take your mate."

I took two steps down and extended my hand to her. Brigid accepted and I squeezed her fingers in thanks.

Once we stood before my father, he proclaimed our union.

"Aodhfionn and Brigid, as much as you have agreed to join as one, we as your clan unite behind you. May you live long, have great happiness, and be well blessed with whelps. By dragon fire, you are one."

I took her other hand and faced her. I had warned her of this part. She nodded and I let my beast come to the forefront, my eyes slit as a dragon. "You are mine," I said and let loose the fire churning in my throat. I did not shift fully, but my scales protected the human side and my snout elongated.

"Your new princess!" My father proclaimed as soon as my fire died down. The clan shouted our moto together and cheered. I took her lips with mine, sealing our union, for my lifetime. Dragons mated for life and mine had just proclaimed her to be his, not something I expected him to do.

Brigid

Aodhfionn led me to the side where his father, mother, brothers, and sister waited for us. The king took my hand and kissed it but said nothing. The drums were so loud I could hardly hear my own voice. The queen embraced me and when she pulled back, I saw her unspoken promise to help me in any way she could. Smiling, I thanked her.

Next were his three brothers. Cahal barely looked at me when he kissed my hand and I felt his slimy lips connect. Grimacing, I leaned further into Finn whose arm came around me. Teyrnon was next and his jovial smile put me at ease. Bearcbhan welcomed me to the family, at least that was what it sounded like but with the music, it was hard to tell. Lastly, was his sister, Tahra. Smiling at her, she took my hand and promised to be great friends.

Once I had greeted everyone in the royal family, Finn's pressure on my back increased and I followed his lead to the side door. As soon as the door was closed behind us, I could hear, the silence deafening and my ears rang.

"I am sorry for all of that, lass," he said. "We have a few moments before the dinner is served. I thought we could use this time to calm our ears from the drums."

"I thank you. It was very loud."

"Aye, dragons enjoy the loudness, it drowns out their inner dragon voices."

"Your dragon speaks to you?"

"More like roars," he answered. "But now, perhaps you will permit me to give you something?" I was about to protest as I had nothing for him, and it wasn't a true marriage. "It is tradition and for as long as you are my wife, this will be yours." He produced the most beautiful necklace I had ever seen. The white gems glistened in the light of the torch. The large emerald hung at the base of the necklace and matched his green eyes and dragon. My breath left me as I stared at it.

"Dear gods that is beautiful," I finally said.

"It is my claim. A symbol to show the others you are mine. It was fashioned when I first shifted, and they knew the color of my dragon. Every male has something made for his future bride. I wanted this. It is yours, Brigid. I ask you wear it to dinner. That is all. You never have to wear it again."

The look in his eyes, reminded me of a young lad when he presented a lady with a favor. I had seen my uncle's son from his first marriage present the current lady with a dandelion when he was five. Finn's expression mirrored the young boy.

Touching his hand holding the necklace, I looked at him straight in the eyes and smiled.

"I love it, Finn," I answered. "I would be honored to wear your claim. Forgive me for not giving you anything."

"You standing as my bride is gift enough," he said. "I thank you for not contesting the marriage. My brother Cahal is salivating for my title. My father is to step down in eight months making me king and I know he would love nothing more than to challenge me. You accepting the marriage gave him less of an opportunity."

"Would he challenge you if he knew…" my voice trailed off.

"That you and I will not be mated in truth?" he finished. I nodded. "Aye, but as no one will know, I believe all will be well."

Finn helped me with the necklace and once it was latched around my neck, he stepped around me to stare at the gem that rested just in the cradle of my bosom. I looked away from his heated gaze but instead of horror at his perusal, I felt a sort of heat that was not all together disconcerting.

"Forgive me," he breathed and looked away. "I have been waiting twenty years to see that necklace around my mate's neck. I did not mean to stare."

"'Tis all right. I am your wife. You have my permission to stare," I said.

"You donnae mean that," he replied. "For staring could turn into something else."

I swallowed but I refused to lower my eyes. "And if it did?" I asked.

"Brigid," he breathed. "I respect your decision and your request. But I beg of you, donnae make it more difficult for me. For I find you excite me in a manner only lovers should. I will reign in my beast, but I ask you donnae make it unbearable. If my dragon thinks even for a moment you are agreeable to be mine in truth, I donnae believe I will be able to stop him from taking you."

At that, I looked down and away from the burning green

of his eyes. When I finally looked back, my eyes were drawn to his and I would have sworn I could see a sort of dragon, pacing behind the green depths.

"Finn," I began. "Your dragon…"

But before I could say anything more, the door opened, and the royal family joined us.

"Forgive us for interrupting you, my dears," Erina said. "But everything is ready for the dinner. They are returning to the Great Hall. Och, look how beautiful Finn's claim looks on you, my dear!"

"Exquisite," Edan replied smiling. "Now come, I know Finn will need some sustenance to be of use to you this evening."

I leaned into Finn when I realized the king's words. He was playing along for the other members of his family. Looking up at Finn, I smiled and kissed him lightly.

"Aye, so I've heard," I replied. "I do look forward to it."

Cahal rolled his eyes and pushed passed us.

"May I ask why he always does that?" I said.

"He lost a female a few years ago and it is his dragon's way of coping," Finn explained.

"Oh my, I am so very sorry for it," I said. "How did she die?"

"She didn't," Bearcbhan spoke up and pulled his wife into his side. My eyes drew to Bearcbhan's mate. She looked away from us. *The randy lad had stolen his brother's female.* "Now, shall we go? I am famished."

Finn held me to him as the others walked on. We were alone for a moment and I looked up at Finn.

"Bearcbhan stole Cahal's mate?" I whispered.

"Aye," Finn answered. "Cahal and Sybine were together for a time, but he never acted on his feelings and when Bearcbhan offered what Cahal did not, Sybine accepted. He is a sneaky one that one, but he loves her and his children to death."

"I must say I'm surprised," I said. "For someone even in my human culture to steal a brother's mate is not done."

"Hence my brother's moody behavior," he replied. "His dragon went rogue for a time."

"Rogue?" I asked.

"Aye, it is when the human side has no control of the dragon. Most go mad. He left the day they asked to mate, and he was gone for a long time. Once he finally returned, my brother was not the same at all. He was growly, irritable, unkind."

"If he was rogue how did he gain control?"

"He is a prince and as such, he has absolute control over his beast... when he wants to."

"How terrible for him."

"I try not to concern myself with their relationship. But they are both my brothers and as such, I worry for them."

"Of course, I understand," I said.

"Well, now that is enough talk of sad things. Shall we go to supper?"

"I confess I am hungry," I said. "But is there anything I should know before?"

"They may ask for a kiss or two," he answered. "Similar to last night."

"I donnae mind that, I have been to a wedding before," I replied. "But what about... later?"

"My father and I have agreed, when I squeeze your hand, you look at my mother and ask to use the privy. She is prepared and will escort you up to my room. After a suitable time, I will sneak out and find my way upstairs without raising suspicion. If anyone makes a fuss, my father will intervene."

I nodded, it sounded reasonable, but I still worried.

"Brigid," his warm fingers lifted my chin to look at him. "All will be well."

I smiled softly at him and agreed. Together, we walked to the dining hall to be greeted by a roar from the clan.

Finn

Brigid looked stunning. Dear gods, tonight would be one of the hardest of my life. I would have to sleep near this beautiful, intelligent, and fearless woman all while keeping my dragon under control. Taking a deep breath, I spoke to him and told him to behave. I would allow him out to hunt later. The beast seemed somewhat content, but I knew it wouldn't last. The faster I could get him out and doing what he enjoyed the easier it would be for me.

Seeing my necklace around her neck, my claim, was nearly too much for me. I had to keep a tight rein on my beast, as his need to claim her was nearly too much. When I slipped her wee hand over my arm, I felt a sense of peace and happiness come over me. Pushing it aside, I walked with her keeping my mind on the evening ahead. Telling my beast it would be better to avenge her, he focused his strength on battle strategy giving me a reprieve from his carnal lust.

We entered the Great Hall to a large roar from the dragons. They cheered and applauded us. Brigid raised herself up to her full height. *There is my warrior queen.* And when the banging on the tables began, she turned toward me. Before I could kiss her, she grinned and threw her arms around my neck giving me a kiss I had never felt before. The kiss of a mate. When she pulled back, she giggled and looked toward the clan. The little human was a good pretender. I saw Cara and Ailidh cheer and smile at her. Shaking myself out of the stupor she induced, I walked her over to my father's table. My family greeted us and soon we were seated together, and dinner was served.

Chapter Sixteen

Finn

Throughout dinner, my eyes kept drifting to my wife. My wife. That was a new saying for me, but for some reason it felt right when it meant her. Brigid laughed and teased my father throughout the evening. My brothers joined in and even my mother and sister teased back. My family was complete. My dragon cooed in the back of my mind as I watched.

Soon, the evening began to drag, and both my dragon and I were getting drowsy. I could only imagine how Brigid felt. Seeing Lir lounging by the fire, allowing my nephews to crawl over him without so much as raising his head, I smiled. Feeling Brigid's hand slip into mine, I looked down and then back into her blue eyes. They were still filled with mirth, but tiredness reflected in their watery depths. Nodding at her silent request, I looked over at my mother who was watching us discretely. She turned to my father and squeezed his hand.

"Forgive me," Brigid said from my side. "But may I use the privy?"

"Of course, dear, I will show you," my mother replied. Both women stood and the men followed suit to show them respect as they left the table. My mother looped her arm through Brigid's as they walked together to the privy and then the back stairs. I took my ale and a healthy swallow, then joined in the conversation.

Brigid

Erina escorted me out of the great hall and down a hallway. Once we were out of view of the clan, she squeezed my arm and pulled me down another hall and then another, coming to the back stairs. With a whispered "quickly", we raced up the stone steps and arrived at Finn's room. Erina unlocked Finn's door and ushered me inside. The sight that greeted me was stunning. Finn's white fire glowed in a gigantic hearth, flanked by two chairs and a large table. His room was nearly three times the size of mine and clearly large enough to fit his dragon form. Candles were lit all around the room and flower petals were scattered on the bed. A large four poster bed with massive oak columns, contained etchings of dragons in various forms and locations. Running my fingers across the etchings, I saw a dragon in flight with fire blasting from his mouth and a young woman tied to a stake. Another etching of a dragon carrying the lass to a castle. And another of a male and female holding hands gazing at each other.

The bed was stunning, but the room was magnificent. "Beautiful," I muttered.

"What was that, dear?" Erina asked from the chest in the corner.

"Just admiring, forgive me," I replied.

"Aye," Erina turned with a nightgown in her hand. "Finn has always been our prince. Cahal is barely a year younger than him, Teyrnon three years and Bearcbhan four. Edan and I always wanted our first born to never have cause to second guess his position. I saw it with my brothers. I have seven brothers and three sisters back in Ireland and my eldest brother, now king of my Irish clan, always worried about his birthright. We never wanted that for our sons."

"I understand," I said.

"Finn will be some time, I ken," Erina said laying out the white silken nightgown on the bed. "Perhaps we could sit and get to know each other? Will you sit with me?"

"I would enjoy that," I answered.

"Some spiced wine?" she offered.

"That would be lovely," I replied. "I never did have any of my own, only as payment for services provided."

"Do you enjoy being a healer?" Erina asked pouring the wine and joining me at the two large chairs.

"Oh yes," I answered. "But I do miss my mother."

Erina took my hand. "What made your clan turn against her?"

"My mother could not save my uncle's wife. She was delivering a child. The baby was breech and my mother was unable to save both. My uncle's wife died, and the child lived but is sickly. After that, my uncle went mad and labeled my mother and I witches."

"Och, he is a simple-minded fool. Edan went to Lewis lands to greet him as the new laird after your grandfather died and saw him strike his wife. Edan called him out on it. Your uncle did not appreciate it and after that, dragons were no longer welcome to trade with the Lewis. Your uncle refused to have Edan there and kicked him out."

"Did Edan challenge him? My uncle had no right to throw the king out."

"No, Edan knew if he would the tenuous peace between

the two clans would shatter. He had more than his pride to worry about. Besides, it is not Edan who was hurt by it and it takes more for my husband's pride to be wounded."

"I must say I am surprised at his reception of me, then," I said. "If my uncle was such a vile man to him."

"Oh, Edan never blamed anyone but Lewis. He would never place your uncle's sins on you. But let us turn our thoughts to happier times."

"Aye," I answered. "I thank you for all you have done for me."

"It is a joy, my dear. My son is my pride and when I heard he was to take a bride; I flew back here with all haste."

"May I ask you about your home?" I asked.

"Of course! Ireland is beautiful. Rolling hills, green meadows, dramatic cliffs with forests and rivers abundant. I grew up in a beautiful land in the western most tip of Munster province of Ireland. My father's line was of the Great Kings of Ireland and even to this day we are heralded as the most powerful. I could speak to you for days regarding my home. But perhaps someday we will visit. I would dearly love to introduce my son's wife to his grandparents." I looked down and into the deep burgundy color of the wine. "No matter how long she may be his wife," she continued.

"I am sure it is a beautiful place," I said.

"Oh, 'tis," she answered. "But when I married Edan and came to Scotland, I saw as much as Ireland is magical, this land... well it is mysterious and mystical."

"May I ask you a question?" something had been bothering me all evening and I did not know how long I had her alone.

"Of course, anything," she answered.

"You may think me strange, but I could swear when I was looking into Finn's eyes earlier today just after our marriage ceremony, I saw a dragon, his dragon, pacing behind his eyes. Was I seeing things, or could I have been wrong?"

Erina leaned back in her seat and stared at me. It was some little time before she answered.

"You were not seeing things, lass," she said. "That is a rare gift to be able to see a male's dragon behind his eyes. Finn allowed you a special glance."

"Do you see the king's?" I asked.

"Aye, I do," she answered. "Now tell me, tell me about yourself. I want to get to know you." Her sudden change of topic worried me. There was something she was not telling me, but I ignored it and began speaking with her.

After several long conversations, I was starting to feel relaxed and tired. Soon, Erina stood and walked over to the bed. Picking up the silken gown, she turned to me.

"Finn will be here shortly," she said. "Perhaps we should prepare you for bed so you do not have to worry about it later."

Nodding, I stood and walked over to her. Taking the white gown in my hand I marveled at the silky feel of it. Erina helped me undress, but when I moved to take off the necklace, she stopped me.

"I know you are not marrying in truth this eve, but dragons enjoy seeing their claim on their mates. It may soothe his dragon for a time. Leave it on and allow him to take it off you," she explained.

I agreed and did not touch it, allowing her to assist me into the nightgown. She was tying the ties, when there was a knock on the door.

"Come in," Erina called. The door opened quickly and was shut just as fast. Finn turned to us and stared at me for a moment. "I will leave you both."

Thanking Erina for her help, I watched as Finn shook his head as if clearing it and spoke low to his mother. He then opened the door and closed it behind her, lowering a beam in the slats to block the door. Then, he turned to me.

Chapter Seventeen

Finn

It had taken me much longer to leave the Great Hall than I expected. All I could think about was my lass above stairs waiting for me. Aye, she wasn't waiting for me in any way I hoped, but still. I couldn't stop my thoughts from drifting to her and my desire to be near her, to hear her laugh, see her smile. My father watched me and when I discretely looked over at him, he nodded once and began a story that had my brother's enraptured.

Sneaking out of the Great Hall, I headed to the backstairs only to be stopped at the base.

"Where do you think you're going, brother?"

Cahal.

Closing my eyes briefly I turned back to him.

"I am in no mood for you," I said. He had left the Great Hall ten minutes before me and I thought I was safe.

"Do you honestly think they would not notice? Your bride leaves under the disguise of going to the privy and is not seen again. Then you sneak out, going up the back stair to... what? See your bride? Do you think the clan would not notice?"

"I care not," he answered. "But I will be going up these stairs whether you *allow* me to or not."

"And what do you think will happen when I raise the alarm? The men want their bedding ceremony."

"An antiquated ceremony for old men and bastards who get their jollies from watching a poor, innocent lass be taken advantage of. If you cannae get your own into your bed, donnae try and watch mine."

His face grew red, but he remained calm. "And when the men storm up the stairs?"

"Raise the alarm, you ken well once I bar the door, no one can come in."

"If you want to be king, you should not change the traditions we have," he threatened. My dragon roared and my eyes turned to slits as I took a step closer to him.

"I *will* be king, and you *will* learn your place, brother. You are a strong warrior and I would be honored to have you in my clan. But until you recognize me as your king, you will nae be welcome in my clan. I will not have someone I cannae trust," my eyes changed back to my human. "Now, if you will excuse me, I have a willing lass waiting for me in my bed, unlike you."

Turning, I raced up the stairs and to my room. Knocking once, I heard my mother call for me to come in. Opening the door, I closed it quickly. Turning to explain my haste and how mother should leave soon, I froze. Brigid stood in a white silken gown, my necklace claim still hanging around her neck. My mother smiled at me, but I hardly saw it.

"I will leave you both," she said softly. I heard Brigid

thank her, but when my mother walked closer to me, I decided to speak with her.

"Mum," I said. She stopped and we spoke low. "I ran into Cahal on the way. He may raise the alarm that we left without the clan's knowledge. Could you speak with Da' about it?"

"Aye, my dear, I will. Your brother is still angry, I am sorry he is taking it out on you."

"At least he fights me with words and not his dragon as he did with Bearcbhan," I said. The memory of their dragons fighting high in the sky after Bearcbhan and Sybine announced their intention to marry was still vivid in all our minds.

"Aye, that is true," mother said. "But let me go down to your father and speak with him now. If something happens, we will handle it, just keep the door bared."

"I will. I thank you," I replied. She gently touched my cheek and smiled at me. Looking back at Brigid, she winked and left the room.

Taking a deep breath, I turned to my wife.

"Is everything all right?" she asked.

I nodded but she deserved the truth. "My brother confronted me on the stair."

"Which brother?" she asked.

"Cahal."

She took a deep breath. "I must confess, of any of them, he is the last I was hoping you would say."

"Aye, I know it," I answered. "But I asked Mum to speak with Da'. Hopefully it will be well."

"Finn..." she started. "If it would be best, I... I will consent."

My dragon roared for me to take her truly, but I suppressed him with a shudder.

"Nay, lass and I beg of you not to say that again," I said.

"My dragon is already clambering to have you."

"Is it painful?"

"To deny him? Aye, very but it would be more painful for me to see the anger and hurt in your eyes, knowing you are trapped and cannae leave because of my inability to reign in my beast. I have made you a promise and I intend to keep it."

She nodded slowly then turned away. My dragon was screaming for me to speak to her. *Why did she turn away?*

"Then what do we do?" she whispered. "If he is to tell the entire Great Hall we have retired, surely they will ask for their traditions to be honored."

"Then we tell them we have already consummated it," I explained. "We have been here for several minutes and I hear nothing yet. I am sure you are very tired, lass. Perhaps we can utilize this quiet moment and attempt to sleep."

"Would you like some spiced wine?" she offered. "It is very good."

"Aye, but perhaps we should get one part of this out of the way in case we do have any late-night visitors," I pulled out my *sgian dubh* and walked to the bed. Pulling down the furs, the white sheets glared at me. Pricking my thumb, I smeared some blood on the sheets and left the furs off the bed. Brigid looked at me confused and my heart sank. I did not think it would be appropriate for me to explain why I did what I did. Hopefully, she would not ask.

"Why did you do that?" she asked, hurrying over to see my thumb. "Och, it still bleeds."

"I am well," I sucked on the wound and soon the bleeding stopped as the wound began to heal. "I heal quickly, lass, if you remember a certain dagger wound..." She looked away and nodded.

"I am sorry about that."

"Och, nay, you were abducted, and a man stood before

you, nude. I would be surprised if you did not attack." I raised my hand. "See? Healed."

She took my thumb and turned it over a couple times. "Fascinating," she replied. "You may make my healing ability unnecessary."

"We still have times of longer recovery," I smiled. "I hope you still wish to practice your healing skills while you are here."

"I would, if that would be acceptable."

"Aye, of course," I answered. "If there is anything you need, we can call our healer and she will give you anything you may desire."

"What I would give for some of my herbs."

My ears pricked up. "What herbs do you need lass?"

"Lavender, Tormentil, I have many at my cottage."

Squeezing her hand, I walked over to my desk and opened the drawer. Producing the pouch, I had the other evening when I went to bring Lir home, I handed it to her. She opened the strings and looked inside. Her gasp and bright smile were enough to melt my heart. I knew then what my dragon had been telling me all along; I would do anything for her.

"You retrieved these for me?"

"Aye, along with Lir."

"Thank you," she looked at me and I saw tears glisten in her eyes.

"You do know I would do anything for you, lass, aye?" She bit her lip but nodded. "Good. Come now, you sleep on the bed, I will be in the chair."

"Nay," she gasped.

"That would be proper lass. I will be well," I promised. She looked at both pieces of furniture then slowly walked to the bed and I watched as she curled under the furs. She did not drop my gaze until she closed her eyes. I took a deep breath, not realizing I held it and turned away from her. Gazing into the fire, I spoke to my dragon.

Brigid

I woke sometime during the night to a sound I did not recognize. Looking over, I saw Finn asleep in the chair by the fire. He looked so peaceful.

Unable to fall back asleep as it was far too warm in the room, I stood and went to the double doors leading to the balcony. Opening the doors, the refreshing breeze cooled me. I stepped out and headed to the stone balustrade overlooking the water. The gentle sound of the waves calmed me.

Then, I heard the same sound that woke me, a soft roar. Looking up, my eyes scanned the dark sky. The ripple was almost indiscernible, but I caught it. A gigantic dark dragon was flying above me. Thinking it was on patrol, I took a step back when it descended and landed on the balcony. The black dragon did nothing except stare at me. Unsure who it was or why they were circling above us nor why they landed, I stood my ground and did not drop the slitted gaze.

Suddenly, I heard a low growl behind me. Jumping and turning, I saw Finn behind me, his own dragon slits staring at the black dragon. My head whipped between them. The black dragon again, did nothing for the longest time. But soon, it crouched and jumped into the air, his massive wings blowing the wind around us. My hair billowed, covering my face. I tried to hold it back and watch, but soon he was gone.

I looked back at Finn, his eyes still slitted. He was watching the now empty sky. Soon his eyes lowered to mine. He said nothing, only turned back to the room and went to the fire. I followed.

"Finn? Who was that?" he didn't answer. "Please."

"Why were you outside?" his voice surprised me. It was

deeper, gruffer.

"I only needed to cool off, it was warm in here."

"It is cold now. Go back to bed."

"Finn?" I questioned. Walking over to him, I touched his arm. He stiffened and turned slowly. His eyes were still slitted. I was speaking to his dragon.

"He is asleep," Dragon said. "He has forced me to swear not to touch you. But I will tell you, you should not be outside by yourself."

"Why?"

"It is not safe. And I cannot protect you if you are not by my side. He has made me swear not to tell you this, but you need to know. We both need you by our side. We can protect you, but we have also claimed you. We both do not want you to leave."

My stomach dropped and my heart raced.

"Now, sleep," he ordered.

"Sleep?" I could not sleep. But his dragon said nothing more and I walked over to the bed. Sitting on the side, I stared at his back. Taking a deep breath, I realized I was not sure if I wanted to leave either. Lying down, I pulled the bedclothes over me and watched Finn standing before the bouncing flames of the fire until sleep claimed me.

Chapter Eighteen

Erina, Queen of the Dragons

"She can see his dragon," I said softly as I lay in the crook of my husband's arm. Edan moved to look at me.

"Truly?" He asked.

"Aye, she asked me what it meant."

"Did you tell her?"

"What? That only true mates can see a dragon behind the eyes? I did not wish to scare her. She's already starting to come around to the idea. She's halfway in love with him."

"Of course she is, he is my son," Edan teased.

I leaned up on my elbow and gazed down at my mate.

"Oh, indeed?" I teased back. "And how long was it until I allowed you my favor?"

"I was a rash lad who needed to be shown that I could not have everything I wanted unless I worked for it. You showed me what a true king was to be, my love and for that I will always be grateful."

I looked down at my husband and a slow grin spread across my face.

"You are trying to earn my favor again, husband," I teased.

"There is nothing I love more than earning your favor, my love, but nay, that was not my intention. I love you and I want you to understand how fortunate I feel being your husband."

My heart melted. The great dragon beside me was mine and mine only. I leaned down and kissed him softly. Just as I pulled back, I stroked my husband's chest.

"I love you, Edan," I said. "Now make love to me."

He gripped me tightly and growled. "I love you. And I will always do as you ask." I giggled as he turned us both to hover over me.

"Careful, oh great king of dragons. I may remember your promise and use it to my advantage."

"From where I am right now, I would say this is to my advantage," he winked and lowered his lips to mine.

Finn

I slowly woke feeling my dragon dosing in the back of my mind. Taking a deep breath, I filled my lungs to capacity and stretched my arms over my head and my legs out in front of me. The chair was not comfortable, but I felt more tired than usual. Looking over to the bed, Brigid lay on her side, curled up with the furs bunched up beneath her arm. I smiled slightly and stood. My usual morning ritual would have to wait as I remembered it was my wedding night last night. Usually, I woke with the sun, walked to the balcony, took in the morning, shifted and flew for an hour. Then started my routine of flight maneuvers and carrying progressively heavier barrels of bags filled with sand. That morning, I walked to the open balcony doors, suddenly confused. I made sure the night before to close and lock them. My head whipped back to the still barred door and quickly prodded my beast awake. Demanding to know what happened, I listened as he explained waking in the chair to seeing Brigid out on the balcony with another dragon.

Possessiveness rushed through me and my immediate reaction was to find Kai and beat him within an inch of his life, but my dragon stopped me with images of the dragon. It was not Kai.

"Good morning," I heard from the doorway. Turning back, Brigid stood behind me, wrapped in my plaid.

"Good morning, lass. My dragon was just telling me about last night's incident. I hope you are well and that my dragon did not hurt or scare you."

"Nay," she answered. "Nothing about you scares me, Finn. I worry is all. Who was the black dragon?"

"Cahal."

I watched as her throat worked around her swallow.

"I am sorry, lass. I will be sure to be more vigilant. I would not have you scared here. I will also speak with my father about his behavior. It was wrong of him to lurk outside our door."

"Finn, I don't think he was a threat. I believe he was... protecting us."

"We do not need him to protect us," I growled. "And do not think he is a friend, lass. He is not to be trusted. He is dangerous."

She nodded but said no more. "Did you sleep well?" I asked.

"I did, thank you," she replied. "Did you? The chair did

not look comfortable."

"I am well, lass."

"I want you to know, I do not expect you to sleep every night for the next three months in the chair. The bed is large, and I do not think I take up much room."

I smiled at her. "Nay, hardly any room at all." Without thinking, I stroked her cheek with my knuckles. So soft.

Her eyes were even more vibrant in the morning like the cloudless sky just as the sun's rays cleared the horizon. So clear, so blue, and so breathtaking. I leaned down to capture her pink lips with mine not caring if I took a liberty. I needed to feel her lips. Just as I felt the barest of touches a gust of wind blew us apart. My brother's golden dragon flew straight up into the sky, belly facing us, as close to the balustrade as he could. He hovered and looked down, a playful look on his face.

"Very funny, Bearcbhan!" I shouted up at him. His dragon let out a choking sound, a laugh, then flew away. Looking back at Brigid I searched her flushed face for a sign I should apologize. Though I found none, I still spoke. "I am sorry, lass."

"Nay, do not be," she said then looked out to the water. "What shall we do today."

"Lass," I pulled her back when she turned to the room. She looked at me questioningly. "If you are... If you are seen outside my room before the sun goes down, I will be a laughingstock within my clan."

"Oh," she breathed. "I had not thought of that."

"I will need to let my beast out to hunt later today. But, if it is all right with you, perhaps we can stay in here for a few more hours?"

"Aye, that would be fine," she answered, then her stomach growled, and my dragon stood at attention. He grew angry with me that I had not seen to her comfort. "Tell your dragon, I am well. Merely hungry. There is some bread over on the table, I will have some of that."

"Nay, lass, I will order one of the maids to bring us something to break our fast. Perhaps some porridge."

"Aye, thank you," she said.

"Of course," I answered heading back inside with her. "Did my dragon speak to you last evening?"

"Aye, he did."

I stiffened. "Will you tell me what he said?"

"Nay, it is between your dragon and me."

"I donnae like secrets, lass," I paused at the door.

"Nay, no secret merely some advice he told me. All is well."

"Verra well," I stated reaching for the door. A knock had me pulling back.

"Finn, Brigid, it's me loves," I heard my mother call softly. Breathing a sigh of relief, I quickly removed the bar and opened the door. My mother stood there with a tray of food. Opening the door wider, she entered, and I quickly took the tray. "I thought you might need something to eat."

"Thank you, I was just going to call for some food," I said.

"No worries, my dear," she answered. "I know you think the clan expects you to stay in bed all day. I will bring up some food or have one of the servants do so later. Is there anything special you would like?"

"I think some mutton enough for a ravenous dragon," I replied telling her of my dragon's discomfort without embarrassing Brigid. "And maybe Lir could join us?"

"Oh yes please," Brigid said. "I do miss him."

"Aye but not yet," my mother said. "I will have him brought up in a little while." She walked over to Brigid and sat with her on the side of the bed. "Are you well, lass?"

"Aye, I thank you. Finn has been wonderful," she replied. "You are truly blessed to have such a son."

My dragon puffed himself up and grinned. I rolled my eyes at the beast.

"I am glad," Mum answered. "But now I must go before I am missed. Stay here for as long as you think necessary. I will bring Lir with me the next time I visit."

"I thank you," Brigid said.

"Thank you, mother," I replied as she stood and walked over to the door.

"Take care of your true mate," she whispered. Her wording caught me off guard.

"My true mate?" I asked. For a dragon to have a true mate, meant they were their one true love and could see their dragon behind his eyes. *Could Brigid be my true mate?* Mum said nothing more only patted my cheek, looked back at Brigid, and winked. She left the room and I again barred the door. Turning back to Brigid, her eyes stayed on mine and then she eventually stood. Walking over to the food my mother had brought, she took one of the plates and began to fill it.

Chapter Nineteen

Brigid

Finn probably thought I was starving. The amount of food on my plate was enough to feed... well a dragon and that was exactly what it was for. It was a wife's duty to serve her husband and as he stood a few feet away from me, all I could think of was his dragon. The beast intrigued me. To be one in the same and yet different, I wondered how he did not go insane. Perhaps later, I would speak to his dragon again.

However much I wanted to speak to him, I did not know what he liked to eat. I hoped he was just as hungry as I was. Then, pouring some fresh ale, I walked back to him with my offering. He looked at the food and then back up at me, surprise registering in his eyes. Without words, he accepted the food but before I could walk away from him, he set the food down and pulled me back. His lips were on mine in an instant and all I could do was fall against him.

Finn

I roared at my dragon. He had taken control and would not give it up. He pushed forward and grabbed his mate to him. The way he was kissing her was certain to make her run, but when she responded and returned his kiss, the smug beast showed me he knew her better than I did. She wanted to be kissed. But when his thoughts turned more carnal, I pushed harder against his hold. I would not allow him to take her without her consent. Not that I believe he would have, but I needed to make sure.

His thoughts consumed him. I was able to break his hold on me and take control. Pulling away as fast as I could, I turned from her. Brigid gasped but I could not look at her. I needed to leave. My dragon was fighting me, and his hold was strong.

"Finn?" she questioned. Turning back to her, she took a step back. My eyes were flashing between human and dragon slits and I was certain my expression was fierce.

"I need to leave," I growled.

"What happened?" she asked.

"My dragon," I stated through clenched teeth.

"Oh," she stepped forward. I raised a hand and stepped back.

"Please, nay, stay," I could barely keep the beast at bay. He wanted her. There was only one way to stop him. Seeing my balcony, I ran and jumped. The beast would not allow me to die. As expected, he shifted, and we flew together. The rush of flying cleansed the lust filled haze and he beat his wings faster. We needed to hunt. We needed to do something other than think of our female who we left, alone, and unprotected.

Brigid

I didn't know what had happened. One moment, Finn accepted my offering of serving him food, the next, he was kissing me harder than he ever had before. Shamefully, I enjoyed it and allowed it, but after a time, he pulled back as if disgusted. My head still spun when he raced out the window, only to shift into his dragon and fly away.

I sat on the chair, my arms wrapped around me and waited. I thought long about what his dragon had said and the more I considered it the more I realized I wanted to stay. But the only way would be to accept Finn as my mate and become a wife to him in truth. Looking over to the bed, I wondered how it would be with him. I was both intrigued and yet nerves set in. Would he want me after or would he take what he wanted and cast me aside? Somehow, I doubted it. There was a knock at the door and I immediately stood. My gaze shifted to the window, and then the bed. Finn's blood stain was visible so no matter who was on the other side, it would look as if we consummated our mating.

Hurrying to the door, I pulled it open coming face to face with Erina, Lir by her side. Seeing my pup, I fell to my knees and held him close. Lir whined and stepped on my lap to lick my face and burrow under my arms. Erina entered and quietly shut the door. I did not realize tears slid down my face until Lir licked them away. I felt gentle hands on my shoulders coaxing me to stand. Erina's soft voice calmed me. We walked to the chair and sat down. Then she went to the side table and poured a cup of warmed spiced wine. She handed it to me and sat opposite me. I took a drink as Lir paced.

"I saw Finn's dragon fly. I wanted to make sure you were all right," Erina explained.

"I don't know what happened," I replied. "I thought I would do a wife's duty and serve him food, but as soon as I did, he… kissed me, then pulled away as if it was disgusting. Then he wouldn't talk to me and he jumped out the window." I looked up at her. "Tell me what happened."

"May I ask a personal question?" She asked. I nodded. "The kiss, was it possessive, demanding, almost harsh?"

The memory of his soft lips pressed firmly to mine, the way his tongue stroked mine, the possessive heat behind his hold on me, hit me as if it was happening again. Looking down, hiding the blush creeping up my cheeks, I nodded.

"I thought so," she sighed. "Brigid, Finn's dragon took over and his desire to possess you caused him to take over Finn's body. I have seen it before. Dragons are very physical creatures and when they claim a mate, they will stop at nothing until that mate is fully theirs. I am sorry. I believe Finn was able to wrestle control back from the dragon and that was when he pulled away from you. It is a very physically painful thing for a human to fight internally against their dragon. That was the look you saw. Then he realized there was only one way to stop his dragon from hurting you and that would be to shift and fly. It is a very scary thing. I am sorry it happened. Have no fear. Finn is strong. He will not allow it to happen again."

"It did not scare me," I admitted. "I have spoken with his dragon last eve. I was concerned for him."

Erina pulled back and stared at me. "Finn's dragon spoke to you?"

"Aye," I answered and proceeded to tell her what happened that evening. Erina listened, then when I finished, she said nothing for a long moment. Finally, she sighed and took a swallow of her spiced wine.

"Brigid, it is time I tell you something important, but I fear your reaction to it. I will have your promise you will hold to your convictions. If what I say causes you to stay here with Finn without truly loving him, I do not believe he will forgive me."

"I promise, your majesty," I swore.

She hesitated again. As much as I wanted to beg her to continue, I kept silent.

"Dragons mate for life."

My body flushed hot then cold as my stomach knotted.

"Finn may have agreed to let you go after three months, untouched, and you would be free to marry anyone you chose, but Finn will never be able to mate another. He may take another to his bed to sire an heir for the clan's sake, but his dragon will never look upon that female as his mate. From what I have seen, Finn's dragon has already claimed you as his. That is why he speaks with you. It is difficult for our dragons to speak. They do not used words often. When a dragon takes over our human side..." She paused a moment, hesitated then seemed to agree with something I could not hear. She closed her eyes for a brief second then when she opened them, they were slitted. Her dragon blinked as she looked at me. It took the beast, still in Erina's form to speak, when she did, it was stuttered and slow.

"Finn... loves... you. That is... clear. His dragon feels... comfortable enough to... speak to you."

"May I ask you a question, Dragon?" I asked. She bowed her head in permission. "Why did he speak to me in such a... rough manner?"

"Because he can't have you," she answered.

"Will he go rogue?" I questioned.

"It is possible," she replied.

I bit my lip as tears pricked my eyes. "What can I do?"

The dragon hesitated. "As it stands... nothing."

"As it stands?" I repeated.

She stared at me, not speaking, but her eyes told me everything I needed to know.

"Become his mate in truth," I surmised. "Stay here."

The dragon looked down, then the eyes changed back to the round of Erina's human form.

"That is not an option," she stated. "As I said, you must stay with your convictions."

"But what if I—"

She raised her hand. "Nay," she stopped me. "Finn made you a promise, lass. I intend to help him keep it."

I realized my argument sounded feeble at best. I would need to speak with Finn when he returned.

"Now, come down and eat with us, we will tell anyone who asks, Finn has a voracious appetite and you needed a reprieve. I beg you to lie about this for Finn's sake. The clan needs to see and hear how their future king satisfied his mate and how virile he is."

I nodded. I would never want to embarrass Finn to his clan. I could draw on some of the gossip I heard when I was in Clan Lewis... It was odd how I did not consider Clan Lewis *my* clan any longer.

Chapter Twenty

Finn

I flew high and fast attempting to wear my beast out. He had very nearly succeeded in taking over and forcing Brigid to be his. I could never let that happen again. If I had to fly to exhaustion every night before I retired, if I needed to be a laughingstock within my clan, then I would. I could never allow her to feel the way she would if I took her as a mate without her truly wanting to stay.

My dragon roared to return, but I kept focused and forced him into submission. He would not use me again. I would not allow it. Brigid's face was burned in my mind, her scared eyes, the look of pain on her face. She did not want me to know, but I had hurt her. The thought of being the meaning behind that look made me roar and the burning acid swirling around my throat expelled as I breathed my white fire.

Still hungry after not having eaten any of the food Brigid

so kindly gave me, I searched out a stag. When I found two, I dived.

My stomach full and my dragon not fighting me every second, I slept in dragon form for a while only to wake when the sun was slipping behind the mountains. It was late. I had left Brigid alone all day. Kicking up a gust of wind, I flew back to the keep. It was past the witching hour when I returned. I hadn't realized how far I had flown. Gently landing on the balcony, I shifted back to my human form and crept inside.

Brigid lay asleep on our bed, Lir tucked in beside her. The deerhound raised his head and growled at me. I suppose the animal instinct he possessed told him I had been the cause of his mistress's distress.

"Easy, lad," I whispered asserting dominance over the animal. "I did not mean to hurt her," He settled. Pulling on a plaid, I sat down by the fire. I would not risk my dragon being so close to her tonight. Closing my eyes, I leaned my head back on the chair and tried to sleep.

Next thing I knew, I heard a loud crash and woke with a start. The dawn light shone down on me.

"I am sorry," I heard Brigid say. My eyes drew to her standing by the wash basin, a shattered pitcher at her feet. Lir scurried past and hid on the other side of the bed. "Lir got into the ash and I needed to bathe him."

"Of course," I answered and only then realized how much I missed her. "Can I help?" I stood, my muscles sore from pushing my dragon the night before.

"Thank you," she paused and looked at me, her gaze unnerving.

"I am sorry if I scared you last morning," I said.

She tried to smile. The side of her mouth ticked up, but it was gone just as quickly. Together we wrangled Lir who clearly did not want his paws and nose washed.

When he padded away to dry his fur before the fire, I looked at Brigid.

"You have nothing to apologize for, Finn. "Your mother explained what happened. I am sorry for my part."

"I would never allow him to hurt you, you know that, aye?" She nodded. "But I had to leave. I will not allow him to claim you. I made you a promise. Perhaps we could make another?"

"What would it be?"

"I will keep my beast reigned in and perhaps, we could not meet as often. For the longer I am with you, the harder it is to keep him contained. If we could simply be part of a clan and go about our duties, perhaps not seeing each other as often, I may keep him satisfied with hunting and flying."

She nodded but the sadness in her eyes ate at me.

"That is for the best," she said. "I will be your wife, but we will be strangers."

"Aye," it destroyed me to say it, but it was needed.

"Aye," she repeated. "I am sorry." She looked away from me and rushed to the door.

I stared after her, my eyes locked on the grain of the oak door. Before she had fled, I swore I saw tears gather in her eyes.

My hands clenched into fists. Just how scared was she? I shook my head. My warrior maiden would not be scared. Something else must have happened.

Cahal.

Had he scared her while I was gone? If he hurt her, I would kill him. Brother or no.

Stalking out of my room, I marched down the hallway

and banged on his door. No answer. Sounds of the males training outside drifted up, I listened trying to see if I could discern his voice.

There.

He was there.

My dragon moved just below my skin. I could feel the scales pricking my flesh. Rushing down the steps, I burst into the bailey.

"Cahal!" I bellowed.

The warriors stopped partly due to my station, but also because they heard the anger in my voice. I was out for blood. My eyes scanned those gathered.

"Show yourself, coward!" I roared. Movement before me caught my eye. He was walking cautiously over to me. My eyes changed to my dragon slits and my teeth elongated ready to sink into his flesh.

"You called, brother?"

His sickening voice made my scales break through the flesh on my arm. Cahal took a stance as if expecting a fight.

"What did you expect to see during your midnight flight? My wife and I intertwined in our bed? Is that the closest you are to the act? You can't have your own female, so you want to watch me with mine? Are you that desperate?"

"No more than you," he shrugged.

I roared and dove for him. My momentum and strength knocked him on his back with a satisfying grunt. Pulling back, I did not give him a chance to move. I threw a punch with my right, then another with my left.

"You dare sneak around and scare my wife? What did you do? You thought you could take a chance while I was gone?"

He twisted beneath me and my next punch hit hard earth as his head moved. Pain radiated up my arm.

Cahal hooked his legs around my waist and an arm around my neck. Twisting, he had me halfway on my back.

"Why did you leave, brother? Answer me that. Admit to the clan you failed to bed your wife," Cahal ordered.

"You all saw the blood stain," I shouted. "Brigid is my mate. My wife!"

"What I saw begs to differ," Cahal whispered in my ear. "And you need to know it was not just me." I grunted but he had me locked. I could not move. "Now what's this about me scaring her?"

"What did you do?"

"Nothing," he stated.

"Liar!" I elbowed him in the side and pulled away then jumped to my feet.

"Careful, brother," Cahal stated, on his feet quick as a wink. "You stole the males' right to the bedding ceremony, now you throw baseless accusations? I would worry some may see you differently."

"You have wanted my title since you returned. Perhaps even before. You are not firstborn, Cahal. The throne will never be yours. You would have to kill me first!"

"I'll take that under advisement," he replied coolly.

I took a step forward, my dragon itching to put him in his place when I heard my father's voice bellow across the bailey.

"Enough!" All eyes turned to him at the top of the stairs. His eyes hard. Kai stood beside him, his rightful place as War Chief. They both moved quickly through the gathered crowd toward us.

My dragon coward at my father's slitted eyes. He was not happy.

"What do you think you are doing?" he hissed, his voice the rough timbre of his dragon. "Has the lass sliced your cods as well as your manhood? Shame on you."

My dragon shriveled into the far corners of my mind.

"Is this what you want our clan to see? Some young whelp who cannae keep his head for a woman? They will nae want to be led by a male who challenges his own brother for no reason. I am ashamed of your actions, lad. Now go back inside. You and I will be speaking again, alone." I bowed my head and, with a glance to Kai, saw his usual stone war face grow harder. I had disappointed my father and my War Chief all due to jealousy and anger. I was better than that.

I had not spent twenty-eight years training to be king for it all to be thrown away. Walking up to the steps of the keep, I stopped when I noticed the women, my mother, Tahra, Sybine, and Brigid standing together watching. My mother's face was expressionless but that was worse than seeing the disappointment I knew lurked beneath the surface. Brigid stood beside her, shock on her face.

I closed my eyes. Today was not a good day. And I had my father's reprimand to look forward to. Without another thought, I headed up the steps to his solar to await my punishment.

Chapter Twenty-One

Finn

My father's mood had not improved by the time he entered the solar. The door slammed open, alerting me to his arrival. Turning to him, I watched as he stalked to the decanter on the side table pouring only one glass. I knew better than to ask for some. But truth be told I was tempted more than once to pour me a large one while I waited the ten minutes for my father to arrive.

"What in the name of the gods were you thinking, Aodhfionn?" my father demanded. "Challenging Cahal in front of the entire clan? Have you lost all sense?"

"I—"

"Save it," he prevented me from speaking. "The only consolation I have in this whole affair is knowing you will punish yourself for your actions far worse than I could. But with that said, you will join Kai scouting our southern most tip of land. You leave in ten minutes. I suggest you go find him."

"I will need to say goodbye to Brigid."

"Nay, you will go to Kai now. One, I donnae trust your dragon to be near her and two that is part of your penance."

"The southern most tip is two days' flight from here. I will be gone five at the very least. You cannae expect me to leave my new bride for that long without saying goodbye."

"I do. You should have thought of that before you challenged your brother for something he did not do. I spoke to Brigid myself. She was not threatened by Cahal. She claims she ran out because she was worried of showing emotion to you. She could not explain her tears and chalked it up to her woman's time but did not know how to tell you."

"Did you speak to Cahal?" I demanded. "Did you ken he landed on my balustrade last evening in order to spy on us? Brigid was letting in some air and he landed right before her. Had my dragon not sensed his presence, who knows what he would have done to her."

"You both have a perpetual need to see the worst in each other. Did it not cross your mind he was protecting you?"

I stared at him incredulously. "Protecting me? We are speaking of the same brother, aye?"

"Donnae snip at me, lad. I am beyond tired of your attitude."

"Cahal has threatened me more than once. Forgive me if I donnae believe he would *protect* me."

My father sighed, the sound one of exasperation. "You are my heir, Finn. Never have you made me doubt that but today I will tell you, you disappointed me."

Those words hit me squarely in the chest. I stared at my father and it was as if a bucket of icy water was suddenly dumped over my head. My sense returned and I immediately knelt to one knee and placed my hand over my heart.

"My king," I spoke clearly. "It is my only wish to make you proud of me. I have disappointed you and by that I have disappointed myself. I am truly sorry for all the distress I have caused you. I am your son and have brought dishonor on your house. I can only offer my deepest regret and apologize. I will do as you request in the hope I may restore your faith in me."

Da' stared deeply into my eyes and I saw the king not the father. Finally, the look broke and he offered his hand to me. Raising up to my feet, he embraced me.

"I have been there, lad," he said. "But as my father warned me, do not allow yourself to be led by *that.*" He nodded pointedly down to below my waist. "You do know she's halfway in love with you already, aye?"

I shook my head. "It doesn't matter, Da'. She wants to leave and as much as my dragon hates it, it is what is. This is what I must do."

My father was quiet for a moment, his eyes searching for something. I wasn't sure if he found it or not but soon he dropped his gaze.

"I should never have allowed you to be the one to take the human mate mantle."

My dragon growled and my father raised an eyebrow. "I am sorry, Da'. My dragon does not understand you. Why?"

"Because... you took her as mate, when she leaves... you will not have an heir. I should have made sure. I should have gone with you and prevented you from growing attached. I should never have allowed you to make that promise. You must have an heir. It is your duty."

"And have I ever shirked my duty?"

"Nay, of course not... I—"

"Love has little to do with siring an heir. When Brigid leaves, I will find a dragonwoman willing to give me a child and

I will do my duty. Have no fear of that."

"Without her? Without Brigid?"

"I have been with many as you well ken, Da'. Aye, when Brigid leaves, she will take a part of me with her, but it will not affect my ability to reproduce nor impair my ability to rule. I will not put that responsibility on her."

"You love her..."

I took a deep breath. "I will not deny it, but I also will not agree. I donnae ken what love is. Let alone if I am able to feel it."

My father's reply was cut short by a knock at the door. Da' sighed and called for them to come in. Kai opened the door.

"Forgive me for interrupting you, my king, but I thought it wise to warn you both. Your conversation is no longer private." He looked behind him. My eyes followed and found Brigid standing beside my mother. She looked up at me and I took note of the look in her eyes. Though it was a strong emotion, it was one I could not discern.

"Erina?" My father questioned.

"Edan," she answered. "Kai told us of Finn's journey, and I wanted to bring Brigid here to say goodbye."

My father said nothing. "Verra well."

I closed my eyes for a brief moment, thankful.

"I will give you a moment alone."

Da' left the room and Kai shut the door. Brigid looked up at me.

"I am sorry," she said.

"For what, lass?" I questioned.

"For not telling you why I ran out and caused you to think... Cahal did and said nothing, none of your brothers did. I merely was... I was..."

"What?" I asked softly.

She wrung her hands and took a shuttered breath. Looking up at me, I finally realized what the emotion was... shame. I took her hands and held them, facing her.

"Did I not promise you in your room and out there," I nodded toward the window. "That I would do anything in my power to protect you? I care for you, Brigid. I ken it's only been a very short time, but I do. I must leave for a mission from my father but when I return, I hope we can speak together? I realize my mother must have told you many things and I wish to discuss them. While I am gone, lass, I beg you... stay close to my mother and do not find yourself alone with Cahal. I cannae protect you and that will bother me more than you ken."

"How long will you be?" she asked.

"Five days at least," I answered. "More likely a fortnight. I shall return for the Yuletide Festival."

She nodded, then another look replaced the shame and it made my dragon sit up and take notice. Her look turned heated and it ignited my need for her.

"I shall miss you," she said.

I had to touch her. Wrapping a stray curl of hair around my finger, I smiled.

"And I you," I admitted.

Before I could realize what she was doing, she threw her arms around my neck and seared her lips to mine. Her touch was hurried and inexperienced, but it made my dragon roar with desire. Dear gods, how was I ever to let her go and when I did, would I not surly die from pain?

I pulled her close to me and returned her kiss, probing with my tongue until she opened for me. I needed her taste, craved it more than my next breath. She gasped as I lowered my hand to her arse and pulled her closer. But she never broke the kiss. I groaned when her little tongue tentatively touched mine. She pulled back but I chased. Just one more taste. She gave in and we intertwined our tongues again. I was in heaven. My dragon cooed in the back of my mind.

Sharp knocking on the door caused her to gasp again and she pulled away. I wanted to kill whoever it was who interrupted. I set Brigid down and held her arms making sure she was steady on her feet before I backed away. If her knees felt at all like mine, she needed the extra support. Her eyes were shining, her cheeks flushed, and her lips were a deep dark red. She looked stunning.

"Come home soon, warrior. I will miss you," she whispered.

A smiled spread over my lips, which ached from the bruising force of our kiss.

"I will come home to you, my warrior queen," I said. "And dream of you every night we are apart."

She smiled and nodded. The door opened and we broke apart. Kai and my father looked at us.

"Ready to go?" Kai asked.

"Aye, I am now," I answered. With a final look at Brigid, I followed Kai to the landing area, shifted and flew south. Brigid's taste still in my mouth, her smell still in my nostrils, and her words still in my mind. I would come home... for her and then we would be discussing her leaving again. Maybe, just maybe, we could make this work.

Chapter Twenty-Two

Brigid

A fortnight later, I woke to the sound of a soft roar and the balcony door opening. Finn's green dragon had landed, and Finn pulled a plaid around his hips. I stood from the bed, Lir by my side and raced to him. He had just shifted and stepped through the door when I threw myself into his arms. He held me tightly to him and I swore he was sniffing me. He took two deep breaths in through his nose and made a soft sigh on every exhale. I kissed the spot on where his jaw met his neck.

"I missed you," I admitted. I was no longer against the idea of Finn being my husband. I realized in the long fourteen days without him, I had never felt so loved, wanted, and happy as I was with him.

His arms tightened around me and his head buried further into my neck and hair.

"I missed you as well, lass," he said softly.

Pulling back from him, I looked into the green depths staring back at me. "Both of you?" I asked seeing his dragon pacing behind the eyes. He stopped moving and looked out at me.

"Aye, both of us."

"I want him to tell me."

"I... I'm no' sure if that is a good idea, lass. He wants... other things. I am keeping him contained."

I felt a blush color my cheeks but held his gaze.

"I admit, I am not ready for... that, though it does not hold the same sort of... disgust I had before." His eyes narrowed questioning me. "I... I know what I said before... but I find I care about you, Finn. I worry about you and I... I think I'm falling in love with you."

I watched as both man and dragon processed my declaration. Having discovered my feelings suddenly over the last fortnight, I could see the same war he was waging within himself. I gave him a moment to process what I said and then continued. "So, I would like to welcome you both home."

It was a risk. But one I was willing to take. His dragon was just as much part of him as a limb. "I trust he will respect me and my wishes to wait a little longer to... be together."

At Finn's dumbfounded nod, I smiled and waited. Slowly, Finn's eyes turned slitted and I raised up on my toes. He was cautious, precious even.

"Welcome home, Dragon," I whispered against his lips and giggled when he growled and pressed his lips firmly to mine.

Throughout the time we were apart, I remembered our goodbye kiss vividly every night and every morning searched the skies for his dragon on the horizon. Every day without him felt like a thousand.

Finally, his dragon pulled back, the kiss not nearly as strong as our goodbye.

"I missed you too," his rough voice said.

"And I missed you, Dragon," I kissed him softly. "May I have Finn back?"

He nodded but smiled at me. Soon his eyes turned back to the round of Finn's human form.

"You spoil him, lass," he teased.

"He's mine to spoil," I said.

Lir whimpered at our feet and Finn broke away from me to bend down and pet Lir's head, scratching behind his ears. I watched loving the view but soon the chilly night air of Yuletide snaked its way down my back, and I shivered in my nightdress. Finn looked up at me and stood.

"Let's get the doors closed, lass, it's cold."

"Will you... Will you sleep beside me tonight?" It was scandalous of me to ask and Finn stared at me for a long moment.

When he finally spoke, his voice was raspy. "Aye, if you desire me to, lass."

"Please," I stated. Finn took a deep breath but slowly nodded.

Together we walked into our room and I slid into the side of the bed I favored. Looking up, I saw the indecision in his eyes as he stared at the empty side of the bed.

"I am sorry to tempt you," I realized what my invitation may have seemed like. "I merely missed you and wanted to be beside you tonight."

Finn nodded. "You are safe from me and my dragon, Brigid."

"I know."

Painstakingly slowly, he went to the other side of the

bed and slid in.

I waited until he was settled and turned on my side to face him. He lay on his back and eventually, he looked over at me. Smiling slightly, he lifted his arm offering. Happily, I moved closer and laid my head on his shoulder loving his arm coming around me, pressing me tightly to him.

We said nothing merely content to hold each other. I did not remember falling asleep only waking feeling the most refreshed I had ever felt.

Looking up, Finn's eyes were closed, and he looked peaceful. I did not move, not wanting to disturb him. Today was the Yuletide Festival, a day I was told were the king's champion was chosen from his guard after battling and sparing with the others of his age range. Finn had never lost, I would have nothing to change that, but it gave me a moment to study him. Could I give myself, heart, mind, body, and soul to the dragonman holding me? The resounding *aye* stole my breath.

Finn, groaned softly, shifted and slowly opened his eyes. He looked down at me and smiled.

"Good morn, lass," he said.

"Good morn," I replied. "Did you sleep well?"

"Aye, I did," he answered. "I feel refreshed from the scouting mission."

"'Tis glad I am. I ken the championship is today."

"Aye," he sighed deeply.

"You will win," I stated.

"I wish I had your confidence."

"You take it with you. I do not need it. I *ken* you will win."

He smiled slightly. "Then I shall win for you."

I smiled and reached up, kissing him gently. Pulling back, I grinned when his eyes stayed closed.

"You must eat," I said.

"I need to speak with my father. Last evening, I came straight here. He does not know I've returned."

"Aye, we will send for him, but you must eat."

He stared at me, incredulously.

"Send... for the king?"

"Aye, he cannae assume you will be able to spar on an empty stomach and from what I was told it starts soon. So, you rest, I will call for food and Edan to be brought."

He stared again, dumbfounded as I got up, pulled on the extra plaid and went to the door.

Chapter Twenty-Three

Finn

Waking with Brigid tucked tightly into my side, all my fatigue from the scouting mission left me. She had welcomed me home like a wife with no one to impress. My heart nearly expired when she asked me to lie beside her. My concern of my dragon taking advantage was unfounded and when she asked to speak to him, he hesitated for the first time. I knew then he would protect her even from himself.

With her promise of a possible future together, both my dragon and I fell into a deep sleep content to hold our mate.

Watching her fuss over me in the morning was endearing but I had already shown my father some disrespect by not going to him immediately upon my return. I could not permit her to have him summoned to our chamber when I was perfectly capable of meeting him in the solar. After a filling breakfast, a deep kiss from my mate and an eager welcome from

Lir, I made my way to my father's solar.

Hearing his command to enter, I opened the door to see Kai standing before my father as if getting more orders. Kai turned and bowed to me before looking back at the king.

"Ah, good morning, Finn," Da' said. "Kai told me he had you check in with Brigid last eve before coming to me. Though I appreciate the sentiment, I would have liked to see you last night. However, I understand the need. I hope your wife welcomed you home properly?"

"Kai knows of our arrangement, my king," I admitted. "There is no need to pretend around him." I had told my best friend of my predicament one evening while we waited for a deer to roast over our fire. Surprisingly supportive, Kai had admitted he knew and the reason he had spoken with Brigid that day a week ago was to be sure we knew someone was spreading rumors. He also admitted, he had not heard if the culprit was in fact Cahal. There may have been another spreading the truth.

"Good," Da' spoke bringing me back to the present. "I assume all was well south."

"Aye," I answered. "We checked in with our farmers and they admit to having been raided a month ago, but nothing was taken. The bandits came in the middle of a moonless night. Rupert heard a muffled banging and went to investigate. He saw nothing out of place. We asked to see the location and he showed us where. I will say it was a little too close to the secret escape route for my liking. We investigated and the actual entrance was undisturbed."

My father's eyes narrowed in contemplation. "We will need to double the guards at night at the Queen's solar. We cannae have anyone ken of that entrance. They would have full access to the keep and all within."

"Aye, my king," Kai bowed. "I will see it done before I go to the festival."

"Good, thank you, Kai. I would like a moment alone with

my son. Go break your fast and I will see you at the festival."

Kai bowed but I knew my best friend well enough to know he wanted to ask something else but hesitated.

"Speak your mind, Kai," I said. My father looked at me but agreed and leaned forward waiting.

Kai looked nervous, more nervous than I had ever seen, and I remembered the day he competed for War Chief.

"Sire, forgive me but... her highness has asked I escort her and stay by her side today," he admitted.

I growled, low and deep. My father held up a hand to stop me.

"Are you telling? Or are you asking?" my father asked.

Kai swallowed audibly, his eyes flashing to me then back to the king. Taking a deep breath, he pulled himself up to his full height, a sign of dominance.

"I am asking your permission to fulfill her desire to be by her side today."

My dragon growled again, and I felt my scales rub against my skin.

"You have it," Da' answered.

"Da'?" I exclaimed. I had told him of Kai's proclivities in the bedchamber and I could not believe he was encouraging his own daughter to be with someone like that.

"My final word on the matter," Da' stated.

"Thank you, sire," Kai bowed.

"I will talk to you more about this later," I mumbled. Kai stopped, turned, and looked at me.

"You are my prince, and my best friend, so I will tell you what I have told no one. You may not like the idea, Finn. And I understand why. Had I seen what you saw and not understood it, I would have acted the same way. I will tell you again as I said that night. She asked me to do that to her. Since then it has never happened again. I would hope you judge me as your friend. I will tell you one last thing that I have not even told your sister... I see her dragon behind her eyes."

I stared at him. That revelation put everything in a new light. Even my dragon stopped. When a dragon shifter admitted to seeing the dragon behind the eyes of another, that was a sign from the gods they were the dragon's best chance of happiness. No dragon wanted to challenge the union since it was so unique.

I searched my friend's gaze, looking for any sign he was lying. I saw nothing but truth. Trying to force my mind to look at him as a potential mate to my sister, and by default a brother to me, I realized I may not be as against the idea as I originally thought. Nodding once, I clapped him on the shoulder.

"You hurt her, I will kill you."

Kai froze a moment, then broke into a wide grin.

"You can try. I'll see you in the sky," with that, he bowed to me, another bow to my father then left the room, closing the door after him.

I looked back at my father, waiting for him to speak. I didn't wait long.

"I am glad you came to the same realization as your mother and I. I will admit, I worried when you told me what happened with the human lass in town. I spoke to him about it. He told me what he told you, apart from the dragon behind the eyes. I made him swear you nor I would ever see Tahra like that. He looked truly horrified. That is when I knew he was a good male for her. He cares for her."

"I see that... now," I admitted.

"And he cares for you," Da' said. "Donnae think I kenned it was not Kai who sent you to Brigid. He may have taken the blame, but the actions were yours."

I could not deny it.

"What is wrong with you, lad?" Da' asked. "Never have I

had such troubles with you. You never rebelled against the rules before. Nor have you acted so selfishly. You always put the clan first until Brigid. Has she weaved some sort of spell over you?"

"She is *not* a witch," I defended adamantly.

"Poor choice of words on my part, I apologize. But what I mean, lad is ever since she arrived you have been different."

"I... I have fallen in love with her."

My father's eyes grew wide and he leaned back.

"And she?"

"Admitted last eve she loved me too."

"You didn't..."

"Nay," I replied. "But I would not doubt it may be soon. She wants to stay."

"Thank the gods," Da' breathed. "I like her, lad and I am happy for you. I hope that means you will have more ability to concentrate on your duties. You have eight months before I step down. There is much to do."

"Must you?"

"Must I, what?"

"Step down?"

A ghost of a mile crossed his lips. "Aye, why?"

"I do not feel ready."

"That is how I know you are, son," Da' said. "I felt the same when my father stepped down."

I took a deep breath and nodded. "Verra well, I will never disappoint you again. I promise that."

"I ken you won't. Not now that you have your mate by your side."

I felt the grin but could not stop it. My father laughed and stood. Pulling me into an embrace, he slapped my back.

"Now, let us discuss what happened and then we will go out to the festival. I will expect you to win again this year."

"You can count on it, Da'," I replied, happy to return to our playful banter. I had missed him.

Chapter Twenty-Four

Brigid

Erina walked with me to the arena, where the dragons were to perform for the Dragon Festival of Yuletide. A time they equated to a new year. The snowcapped mountains were before us and the wind was chilly but not biting. Erina led me to the family booth and I sat beside her on her left, her daughter to her right. The men were to shift and spar with their opponent's dragons, the best winning the title of the king's champion and a kiss from the lady of their choice.

"I am excited to see Finn spar," I leaned over to say, my eyes on Finn speaking with Kai. After we ate breakfast, Finn left to go to his father. Edan offered to come to our room but Finn wanted to show his respect. I dressed with Sara's help and found Erina and Tahra.

"Aye," his mother answered. "He has won it the last two years."

That made my heart race with a question. "Who did he kiss those last two years?"

Both Erina and Tahra looked at me and smiled.

"You did not think that you were the first lass he kissed, do you?" Erina teased. "But rest assured you are the only one he will kiss this year."

"If he wins," Tahra replied. "I think Kai has a good chance of winning this year."

"You say that every year, love," Erina smiled. "But perhaps you are right. Kai is a strapping young man and his dragon is fierce."

"Aye," Tahra answered, her eyes falling towards the handsome captain of the guard and my husband's best friend.

Leaning further into Erina, I whispered, "Is there something going on between them?"

"Aye, the young lass thinks her father and I donnae know, but we've noticed it."

"And is it unrequited?"

"Kai is a very quiet man when it comes to Tahra, but his dragon sings for her. A woman knows that look."

I looked down. I did not know the look she meant. But then my eyes turned to Finn and I caught him watching me and a slight smile lifted one side of his lip, but the same heated fire reflected in his eyes. That look. I smiled widely at him and blew him a kiss. I kept my eyes on his until he was pulled away by another.

Looking back at Erina, I saw her watching me intently. Before she said anything, a cheer rang out and the King stepped forward.

"Dragons," he bellowed. "It is with great pride that I announce the opening of the Yule Festival!" Deafening cheers rang out from the crowd. "As every year, our dragons must prove who among us is the best warrior. And as I am sitting out this year, again," he teased. "It will be difficult to choose who is the greatest." A general chuckle came from the dragons around me. "But," he continued. "I know my eldest son, Finn will not disappoint me. All of my sons are strong warriors, a tribute to their mother." Erina laughed. "But as my heir, Finn... we are all watching for you."

"As I will be getting a kiss from my wife, my king, you can count on it!" Finn answered back.

"If that's the only time his wife kisses him, you had better worry, your majesty!" Kai called.

"Shut it, ya wee glop or I'll finish you off first," Finn replied.

"I would like to see you try," Kai prodded.

"Now now, keep the rivalry until you are in dragon form," Edan called back laughing. "Let the games begin!"

Another cheer rang out and flute and drum music began. Several dragons shifted and lifted off the ground. The king walked to the family booth and kissed his wife.

"You best remember what you said, lad," Erina teased. "I may have to remind you of that later."

"I look forward to it," he winked and sat down between his wife and daughter. "Are you excited to see your first Dragon Yule Festival, lass?" He asked me.

"Aye," I answered. "It is fascinating."

"'Tis," he replied and took his wife's hand in his resting it on his lap. "Donnae worry, lass. Finn will win."

"I donnae doubt it," I said. As I watched two dragons fly above us, ramming into each other, the sparing began.

Finn

Dragons sparred high above me and my dragon was

itching to join in, but I had to wait for my age range. Bearcbhan won for his age of twenty to twenty-five. Next year, he would have to join Cahal and me in the twenty-six to thirty-year-old warriors. I glanced at my brother. The stoic Cahal looked away when Bearcbhan claimed his victory kiss from his wife. Cahal remained in the clan for my parents' sake but when they passed on, I doubted he would stay. As much as I watched myself around him, I worried about his motives and the rogue dragon he tried to restrain every day. I missed the old Cahal. The one I grew up with. He was my best friend. He, Kai, and I were all around the same age and I missed our old confidences, our sparing sessions without thinking he was honestly trying to kill me, and the times we would go to the small island in the sea, hunt a stag, drink, and talk. It had been years.

As the clan herald called for a pause between tournaments and music ensued, I prepared my dragon for the fight. Looking around for Teyrnon, I hadn't seen him all day. He usually enjoyed the tournament. It was not required to participate but he usually did. My eyes found him sitting near our mother, his arm wrapped in strips of plaid. My brows furrowed. He had wounded himself. I would need to speak to Brigid. I worried for him but when he caught my gaze, he smiled, waved, then motived to his arm and rolled his eyes. Nothing bad then. Good. I gave a nod and my eyes moved to my wife. She was sitting on the other side of my mother. I smiled as she spoke to my sister. I felt a sort of peace descend. Hopeful for the future, I turned my attention to my first competitor, a dragon just out of the previous tier. It didn't seem fair and the five minutes it took for my dragon to defeat him was not nearly enough. The clan cheered when the dragon bowed and conceded me as winner. Landing, I stayed in dragon form, waiting for the next fight, and again my gaze drifted to Brigid.

Her eyes were fixed on my dragon's green hide. The beast puffed himself up and watched as her eyes danced and she smiled.

Easy, I cautioned when my dragon began thinking of all the ways to make her smile. The beast ignored me and continued. I growled when his mind turned to a more physical bent. *Not now. Focus on the task at hand. Cahal would love nothing more than to beat us.*

My dragon snorted and shook his massive head. When my name was called opposite Kai, I grinned and stretched my wings. This would be fun.

Brigid

I watched as Finn's green dragon and Kai's blue one leapt into the air. Both men were a beautiful sight as their dragons blew out fire, Finn's white and Kai's blue mixing together. The second Kai barreled into Finn's chest, my heart stopped momentarily.

Their fight was by far the most intense but after a while, I noticed Finn's tactics change slightly. It was almost as if he was toying with Kai. Kai would barrel into him and he would fly higher, causing the blue dragon to miss his mark and spread his wings to stop himself. Kai turned back around to Finn and if dragons could grin, Finn would have. Kai snorted out some smoke and they circled each other. Kai tried another barrel roll, but Finn again moved away, this time with a small fire ball landing right on Kai's bum. The blue dragon yelped and turned sharply. Kai raced towards him, but Finn climbed higher in the sky, faster and faster into the crystal clear blue.

Kai slowed down and roared after Finn. Finn's dragon looked back and after a second, changed course and raced down to Kai's chest, successfully pushing him quickly to the earth. Kai spread his wings, but the wind and Finn's sheer size was too much. At the last second, Finn twisted and they both landed on the earth with a thud. A cheer rang out as Finn was announce that round's winner.

Staying in dragon form, Finn spread his wings and raised himself up to his full height. His massive head swung to look over at me. I cheered with everyone else, but the look in his dragon's eyes made me want to cheer my dragonman on even more.

Chapter Twenty-Five

Finn

Kai was easy. We had sparred together since we were lads. When he made his signature mistake, I took it to my advantage and used it against him. The rest was just for fun. I wanted to make a show for the clan. They always enjoyed a good sparring.

Resting for a time, the next fight I had was with an older dragon, albeit by a couple years but even one year older slowed a dragon. He was a quick defeat but still it primed my already warm muscles because the next and final opponent, was my brother. Cahal. And as I came down to land, I saw Cahal watching my every move with territorial and feral eyes.

Stretching his black dragon, we faced each other and waited for the herald to announce our final round. Fire flashed in Cahal's eyes and I knew what he was thinking. It was the last round of the day. We were the final two warriors... and he had never beaten me. We had battled about ten dragons each in order to face each other and he was hungry for victory. A victory he would never have. There was no way I would allow him to win. My dragon agreed and for once it was not because he wanted a kiss from Brigid, but because he knew his place as heir. If we lost, the clan could side with Cahal as king.

My eyes turned to my father and I saw his almost imperceptible nod. He knew I would win. And I would not let him down. With a final glance at Brigid, she bit her lower lip seeing the exchange between my brother and me. I would win. For her. Tiredness be damned. This was a battle I *could* not lose.

Brigid

The herald announced the battle, and immediately Cahal's black dragon leapt into the air. Finn followed but the more he climbed, the more I worried. Cahal had murder in his eyes. Finn stopped and coasted on his back, wings outstretched, almost as if he sensed something. Cahal turned suddenly and barreled down to Finn, but my dragon had anticipated it and dodged to the side. The black dragon roared and blew his red fire at Finn, catching his back legs. Finn let out a yelp and tucked his legs under him. Taking the advantage, Cahal tackled him.

"That is not fair," I stood up and shouted. "Are there no rules against that?"

"What makes that so different from what he did to me, lass?" Kai asked from his seat beside Tahra. "His fireball landed on my arse."

"Language around my daughter, Kai," the king snapped.

"I am sorry," he looked down then to Tahra, who smiled.

"There are no rules in dragon sparring, lass," the king explained. "If I feel they stop sparring and begin fighting in truth, I will intervene, but not until that time."

"He wants to kill Finn! Did you not see the look in his

eyes?" I cried.

"Brigid," Erina calmed me. "Finn will be fine. He has never lost to Cahal yet. He will not lose this time."

"But look at him!" I cried, not realizing tears were gathering in my eyes. Cahal struck at Finn, catching him on the side of the eye. Finn's dragon whimpered as blood dripped to the ground below. "Finn!" I shrieked.

He looked down at me and I placed my hand over my heart. His eyes twitched for a moment then, he looked back at his brother. Kicking Cahal straight in the gut with his powerful hind legs, Cahal flew off him but caught himself by spreading his wings. Both dragons flew at each other, but Finn looked more determined than I had ever seen. The brothers embraced. Finn gripped Cahal's neck and twisted, latching on his back. The black dragon flailed and tried to grab at him to no avail. Finn raised his hind legs, without letting go of Cahal's neck and beat his massive wings, forcing Cahal to fall fast from the sky. Cahal roared and let out another gust of fire before Finn successfully forced him to land, with him on top.

The crowd was silent. But as soon as the dust settled and the green dragon was shown victorious, a loud cheer rang out. Finn shifted back to his human form, wrapped a plaid around his waist and allowed his arm to be raised as victor.

Cahal huffed some grey smoke and jumped into the air. Finn caught my eye as I cheered for him and raced to me. Jumping up and sitting on the edge of the booth, he caught me around the waist and pulled me to him. Blood trickled down from a cut above his eyebrow, but I didn't care. Grasping his face in my hands, I kissed him. The awkward angle gave us pause but as soon as his lips touched mine, all other thought left me.

My dragonman was victorious.

Chapter Twenty-Six

Finn

The celebrations continued well into the night, but I grasped Brigid's hand and squeezed her fingers. Fighting that day had worn me thin and all I wanted was to climb into bed and sleep. As I rose, about to take my leave, Brigid stood with me and wrapped her arm around my waist. She had been the perfect wife that day; fussing over me for the clan to see and staying by my side. I looked forward to some alone time with her, perhaps we would be able to repeat our previous evening; kissing well into the night.

"Are you leaving us so soon, brother?" Bearcbhan teased. "It is not as if you did anything today."

"Aye, ya brat," I replied. "And besides, I have a beautiful wife I need to thank properly."

Brigid pulled me tighter to her. "And I have a victorious

warrior to take care of," she whispered. Her voice husky, I swallowed and cleared my throat.

"Be sure to give him a thorough examination," Bearcbhan called after us.

"Have no fear, Bearcbhan, I intend to," she answered.

Turning amidst bawdy shouts and lewd cheers, I took her arm and escorted her up to our room. Once we were alone, I shut the door and watched. Brigid walked to the side table, pouring two cups of whisky. Without another word, she handed me one and pressed on my chest, as if asking me to sit. She knelt before me and assisted me with my boots.

Once I was comfortable, she smiled at me and went to the hearth to stoke the flames. The fire roared to life. Turning back to me, she said nothing, but her hand moved to the ties of her dress and slowly, with shaking fingers she loosened them. My dragon, the sleepy beast, immediately looked up and took notice.

"What are you doing?" I managed to get out when I saw she was pulling off her outer gown.

"Shh," she whispered. Suddenly, the room felt very warm and my hand clutching the cup began to sweat. My eyes were riveted by the sight of the most beautiful woman I had ever seen, slowly removing her clothing.

After a little while, she stood in her shift, so thin with the fire behind her, I could see the outline of her body. Her hand moved to the pin holding her hair. Pulling it out, the red locks fell around her shoulders in silky waves. My hands itched to touch it.

"Brigid," I choked. "I," she stepped forward and placed a finger to my lips. My dragon roared at me to stop speaking and let her continue but it wasn't fair to her. Or me. She was tempting me with something I did not know if I could have. "Are you sure?" I asked when she removed her finger.

"I want to," she replied. "I want you, Finn. I want to be a

proper wife to you. You have proven you are a good man, an even better warrior, and someone I am proud to call my husband. You never forced me, though it was your husbandly right. You have been so kind to me. But now I find I yearn for more. I want to know what it is to be yours. I want you... I love you."

My breath caught and my dragon fell silent. Never had we heard those words from a female and in that moment, I knew I would never want to hear it from another. She took a step back and loosened the ties of her shift. The flimsy material fell away and my wife stood before me unabashed in her beauty. The firelight danced on her creamy skin.

I stood, set the whisky aside and walked to her. Before I stood too close, I went down on my knee to pledge to her. "My wife," I started. "You give me a precious gift I cannae return. The gift of your innocence. But know this; from this day forward, you and only you will share my bed, my life, and my love. There has never been a female before you who has made me feel this way. You become my mate this evening. I want you to know, I cherish you and care for you. As your husband, I promise to honor you, listen to you, and keep you by my side. I vow on this day, you are my equal, my queen, my wife, and my mate. Brigid, I love you."

Brigid

My hands shook when I first pulled the ties of my gown but when I saw the look in my husband's face, all my fears fell away. His eyes flashed to dragon slits when I stood in my shift and my thoughts went to feeling his hands in my hair. Unpinning the heavy mass, I let it fall and smiled inwardly when I saw his eyes grow heavy.

Finally, I stood nude to his perusal and never had I felt so alive. Finn's eyes trailed over me, causing a hot flush to raise my skin. He stood and knelt before me, vowing everything I ever wanted. Tears pricked my eyes when he told me he loved me.

My one thought echoed back to my ears as I said; "Make me yours, mate."

Standing, he pulled off his tunic in one swift move. Hope flare within me. His tanned skin contrasted the white fire within the hearth as the flames flickered making his skin glow. He stood before me in only his kilt.

I took a step towards him and reached for the belt that held his plaid around his waist. Taking the end in my hand, I unhooked the leather but paused. Looking up into his eyes, I was more confident than before. As I gazed into the green depths, seeing his dragon watch me, my decision was made.

"Make love to me, Finn."

Before I could release the leather of his belt, he pulled me to him. Our bare torsos meeting for the first time and the feeling of his chest against me caused me to gasp as he rammed his lips onto mine. My hands left his belt to bury in his brown hair. His plaid falling away, we both stood naked within each other's arms. Lifting me, I allowed my instinct to rule, and I wrapped my arms and legs around him. He walked me to the bed and slowly, gently lay me down. No fear entered my mind, only love for the dragon and man hovering over me. My husband, my love, my mate, my heart of fire.

Chapter Twenty-Seven

Brigid

I slowly woke to the sun shining down on me, wrapped in strong arms and pressed to the body I had spent all the night before examining in minute detail. My husband held me close to him, the soft rise and fall of his chest lifted my head. Taking a moment to myself, I recalled all that had happened the night before. Finn had been so gentle and loving I had felt like a queen. His queen.

My fingers toyed with the soft hair on his chest and I placed a gentle kiss on his shoulder. My dragonman sighed and shifted but did not wake. I laid my head back on his chest and took a deep breath.

I was home.

As much as I hated my uncle, I found myself thanking him for choosing me to marry this amazing man.

The next time I opened my eyes, it was because something shifted under my head. Looking up, Finn gazed down at me with a soft smile.

"I did not mean to wake you," he said quietly.

"I'm glad you did," I replied, leaning up and kissing him.

Pulling away, I smiled when I saw his eyes were still closed. When he opened them again, all I could think about was him staring down at me last night as he made love to me over and over again.

"How are you feeling, lass?" he asked softly.

"Well, verra well," I answered. "You were so loving."

His lazy smile lifted a corner of his lip as he buried his hand into my hair and pulled me down to his chest again.

"My wife," he said quietly.

"Are you trying to convince yourself? Or do you say it only because you are surprised?" I teased.

"I am trying to convince myself," he answered. "It feels as if it has been such a long time. I am trying to believe it finally happened."

"As am I," I replied. "I enjoyed every moment of it. It is true what Cara and Ailidh said."

"Oh? What did they say?" he asked.

"Dragons are highly skilled in the bedroom."

He grinned, moved to his side, flipped me on my back and leaned down to kiss my neck. "That's right, lass. Highly skilled in loving our mates."

"A fact I am pleased to have learned firsthand."

He said nothing as he loved me with every fiber of his being. I felt his possession down to my toes. I was his just as much as he was mine.

When we pulled away from each other, I laid my head on

the pillow, him resting beside me; watching me.

"I know we have duties, but I find I do not want to leave."

"Neither do I," he said softly.

I could not hold in my giggle. Burying my face into my hands, I laughed.

"Laughing at your husband after he makes love to you is not exactly what he wants to hear, love," Finn grinned.

"I am sorry," I replied. "But I was not laughing at you. I was thinking about... us."

"What about us, love?" he asked.

I looked down, almost embarrassed. *How could I admit what I was thinking about?*

Finn

She looked so adorable looking down and attempting not to tell me what she was thinking about. Though I knew, because I was thinking the same. Without answering me, she leaned away and eventually stood. Taking the plaid, she was about to wrap it around her body when my dragon whined.

"Don't," I said. "My dragon does nae want you covered up."

"I'm cold without being beside you," she replied, her face falling.

"So am I," I answered. "I do not want you cold, lass. Cover up and then come back to me quickly. My dragon has plans for you," I winked.

She smiled seductively, wrapped herself in a plaid, and hurried to the door of the privy. Laying back, I placed my forearm over my eyes and sighed. My dragon snoozed in the back of my mind as happiness and peace encompassed him. He had claimed his mate the night before.

There was a knock at the door and, looking towards the privy, I stood, found my kilt from the night before, and wrapped it around my waist. Opening the door, I came face to face with my father.

"Da'," I smiled. His eyes passed over me then over my shoulder to the bed. I knew what he saw without turning.

"Finn," his voice was low. "What happened?"

"I donnae think I need to say, Da' you can see, and I will not embarrass my wife by telling you everything."

"Careful, lad," his voice was soft but still disciplining. "What about the agreement?"

"It was an agreement until she wanted me," I explained. "And last night, she asked to become my wife in truth."

"And you allowed it?" he asked.

"There is little a man can do when his wife is offering herself to him," I answered. "I donnae understand why you are concerned about this, Da'. You and mother waited until she was ready. I spoke to you about this earlier."

"There is more going on, lad than you know," he sighed.

"Such as?" I asked. "As your heir, I should be kept informed of something that may affect the clan."

"Come to my solar and we will talk more," he said.

"Finn?" I heard behind me. Brigid had come out of the privy, wrapped in a plaid. When she saw my father standing in the door, she clutched the plaid around her firmly.

"'Tis all right, love," I replied. "Da' was just telling me something that's happened."

"Something bad?" she asked.

"I donnae ken," I answered. "But he asked me to his solar."

"Then you should go," she replied. "Forgive us for sleeping in so late, your majesty."

"Lass," Da' said. "You ken I asked you to call me Edan and now that you are married in truth, I insist upon it."

She blushed and looked down. I would have closed the door on my father for embarrassing her, if it had not meant disrespect.

"Give me a few moments to dress properly, Da' and I will meet you in the solar," I said.

"Aye, but I need to speak with you urgently," he replied. The hidden message was clear, *do not take time with your wife.* As he turned away, I closed the door and looked back to her.

"What do you think is happening?" she asked walking over to me.

"I donnae ken," I answered, taking her in my arms. She laid her head on my chest and sighed.

"I wanted to spend the day with you, here," she murmured.

"We still can," I answered. "Let me speak with my father and we will be able to be together. I will bar anyone from needing me."

"You have duties."

"My first duty is to take care of my wife," I said kissing her nose.

"And you did, all night and this morning," the minx replied, gazing up at me. My dragon roared in agreement, urging me to ignore my father and love my wife. "Tell your dragon to wait. There will be plenty more times for us. And I intend to speak with him again." Again, the beast roared so loudly, I winced. "What is wrong?"

"Nothing, just my bloody beast begging me to stay with you so he can have his fun."

"Tell him, go to your father, then return to me. I will reward him for his patience," she winked.

"Och, lass you donnae know what you are doing to me,"

I said, leaning down to kiss her. Neither of us pulled back for a time until someone pounded on the door.

"Finn, ya bloody bastard, get your arse out of bed and get to the solar. Da' is waiting for us."

"Bearcbhan," I snarled.

"Aye, lad, let the beautiful lass be. She needs her rest," Teyrnon spoke next.

"Go, before they break the door down and see me in nothing but your plaid," Brigid said.

"No one but me will be seeing you in nothing but my plaid, lass," I replied. "But I should go."

"Finn," they yelled and pounded again.

"Shut your gob, lads, I'm on me way," I shouted back.

Looking back at Brigid, I leaned down and gently kissed her again, not trusting myself with any more than a brief kiss. Brigid pulled me back and kissed me deeper. I didn't want to let her go, but when my brothers tried the door handle, I pulled back quickly. No other male would see my wife, my mate not properly dressed.

"I should go," I said. She nodded and stepped away. Tightening the kilt around me, I looked for the belt. Brigid found it and offered it to me.

"It is my duty to dress you," she said. "Please allow me?"

My throat closed for a moment. I had never had a female dress me before. Never thought I needed it or wanted it but the look in her eyes as she wrapped the leather around my waist and assisted me with my tunic and fly plaid, took my breath away. It was only a short time later when she ran her hands across my shoulders and into my hair. Her beautiful blue eyes glittered with love.

"Now go, my dragonman," she said. "But hurry back to me so that I may keep you in our bed all of the day."

Growling, I pulled her closer and kissed her. My brothers

again banged on the door.

"Damn them," I grumbled. Brigid giggled and released me.

"Go now, before they go without you.

"I don't understand why Da' called us all," I shook my head.

"It must be important," she said.

"I will be back shortly, love."

"I will miss you," she answered. Placing a quick peck on her nose, I moved to the door.

"Move that way, love," I motioned. "I don't want them to see you." She laughed but did as I asked and moved out of the line of sight of the door.

"I love you," she called.

I stopped and looked back at her. "I love you." With those words in my head, I pulled open the heavy oak door, my brothers' grinning faces greeted me. I growled.

"I would much rather have stayed with my mate than to see your smiling mugs," I grumbled.

"Mate, is it?" Teyrnon asked. "It's about time you mated her in truth, brother."

"What do you mean?" I demanded. "I mated her on our wedding night."

"Aye, no one believed that small drop of blood, Finn," Bearcbhan replied. "Thumb was it?" he teased. "And then of course you flew away."

"Let alone your short temper and the need to fight Cahal... Though I understand that," Teyrnon said.

"Don't know about you but my female never let me out of our bed until dawn the second day. And I can assure you, she slept little those nights."

"Not that I care what you did with your wife, Brother, I demand to know who is spreading such a dastardly rumor. Brigid is my wife."

"Aye," Teyrnon answered. "But we all knew you would never force an unwilling lass."

"We are happy you have your mate in truth," Bearcbhan said. "We were getting tired of the façade. So, tell us, Brother how was it? How does it feel to be mated to your female?"

"Brigid is my wife and your future queen, you will show her some respect," I snarled.

"Och, come now," Teyrnon said. "What kind of brothers would we be if we did not tease you?"

"Better ones," I ground out.

"Och, I tell you all about me and Sybine," Bearcbhan answered.

"Aye and none of us want to hear it, Cahal least of all. I donnae ken why you torture him so," I replied.

"Who speaks for me?" Cahal's voice came from the darkness at the top of the stairs. He came into the light of the window. We all fell silent as we climbed the steps to our father's solar.

"It must be important if Da' called us all here," Teyrnon replied.

"Aye," I answered. "He said it was something that could harm the clan."

"In that case," Bearcbhan replied, suddenly serious. "Let us go in."

Chapter Twenty-Eight

Brigid

Looking around the room after Finn left with his brothers, I did not know what I should do. I had already made the bed, though I stripped the sheet and crumpled it up, stuffing it inside one of Finn's wardrobes. I needed to ask him what we should do with the incriminating evidence. Perhaps he could burn it up with his dragon fire that way no one know we had only just consummated our marriage.

Taking a rag, I began wiping the surfaces of the furniture down to clear them of dust and grime. As warm as dragon fire made the room, the soot reached everywhere. Opening the balcony doors, I breathed in the crisp air. There was a knock on the door distracting me from my thoughts.

"Who is it?" I called, still unsure of anyone but the royal family and even Cahal was one I watched.

"'Tis Tahra and Lir," the princess's voice was muffled through the door, but I smiled and opened it. My pup barked when he saw me and bounded over, nearly knocking me down.

"Lir," I laughed and petted the dog's head. Tahra giggled as the pup licked my face.

"He is adorable," Tahra said. "I have asked Papa to get us one. Maybe they will be best friends."

"Would you like that, Lir?" I cupped my dog's face in my hands. "A friend to play with?"

The pup's soft bark was answer enough. I laughed and looked up at my sister by marriage.

"I thought you might like some company," Tahra replied. "I am supposed to be at my studies but Teyrnon was pulled away by Bearcbhan. They were to meet Papa in his solar, so I found Lir lounging by the fire in the kitchen and had him come with me."

"I'm glad you did," I said. "How is Teyrnon's arm?"

"Fully healed. He could have sparred yesterday but was worried about losing and looking weak," she giggled. "My brothers are funny about that. But I do feel horrible. My brothers are all sweethearts with me."

"He offered to teach you. I am sure he isn't upset. You only dropped him a little way."

"But enough to break his arm."

"Och, if I told you how many times I hurt my father when he was training me, you would be amazed."

Tahra paused. "You never speak of your parents."

"The memories are too raw, I cry each time," I admitted looking down.

"Oh, donnae do that! Would you like to go on a walk?" she changed the subject. "'Tis quite temperate out."

"Lovely idea," I replied. "Let me get a cloak."

"Aye, I need one too, I will meet you at the kitchen?"

"I will be quick," I smiled at her.

Finn

"Bastards," Bearcbhan muttered after Da' told us his news. "What the bloody hell do they expect us to do? *Not* rescue our females?"

"We must not be rash," I said. "We donnae ken if they're alive or dead. We need to send a scouting party and see what we can."

"That Lewis bastard has crossed the line twice now," Cahal replied. "First with giving Finn an unwilling lass and now this."

"Brigid is not unwilling, and I'll thank you to keep a civil tongue in your head when you speak of your future queen," I spat.

"She is nae queen to me," Cahal answered.

"Then you turn your back on your clan when I become king," I replied.

"I am loyal to my king and you are not my king," Cahal said then looked back at da'.

"Enough," Da's commanding voice shook the roof. "Finn is my successor, Cahal and no matter how much you covet it and your other brother's mate, you will have neither. You are my son and I love you, but you should think before you speak. You will never be king, and it is high time you accept Aodhfionn's position." Da' never used my full name unless it was for a specific reason. "If you cannot do that, then tell me now and save your mother and I the heartbreak of your disloyalty."

Cahal stared at our father. As rash as he was, I knew he would never hurt Da'. For one, Da' would never allow it, he would shift and Cahal's black dragon would be dwarfed by his red one.

"You, as always, Father have my loyalty," he replied. "My rashness was directed incorrectly."

"'Tis not to me you should pledge," Da' answered. Cahal looked over at me. I pulled myself up to my full height. I was taller than all my brothers but Cahal came closest at only two inches shorter than my six-foot four-inch frame.

Cahal sucked his teeth and took a deep breath. "Aye, you have my loyalty too," he grunted.

"That halfarsed pledge will not work when I step down and he leads the clan. I expect you all to take out your daggers and pledge to him," Da' said.

"Da', forgive me," I replied. "But we are wasting time. Our females need rescue. Permit me to gather a scouting party and let us fly to Lewis lands. We will look for any sign of them. Once we find them, we will report back."

"I also want to know how they were able to sneak up on our women. Where were the guards?" Da' questioned looking at Kai at his side.

"I have them in holding. I intend to question them," Kai stated.

"I will assist you," Teyrnon said.

"Do you not think it prudent to gather a force against these humans? Aye, get a scouting party together but have our army waiting in a nearby glen so if you find our females you can send one of your party back to tell us and we can waste no more time in rescuing them," Bearcbhan offered.

For all his teasing and pomposity, Bearcbhan was a strong strategist, even at his young age of twenty-four. I looked forward to having him by my side when I became king.

"Aye, good idea, lad." I looked at my father and he continued. "Take a few dragons you know are loyal, with you and have your three brothers rally the army. Bearcbhan, since it was your idea, you lead the men to victory."

Bearcbhan's eyes lit up. Even in his early twenties and a father, he was still a boy.

"Aye, Da'," his voice was light. "I will not make you regret your decision."

"I ken I won't, lad," Da' said. Cahal's fist clenched at his side and his eyes flashed to slits. He was not happy with our father's decision to have the youngest lead the army.

Da' dismissed them all but called me back to him. "Shut the door, lad." I did and stood before him. "I ken I was gruff with you earlier. I am sorry. I am very happy for you and the lass. Brigid will make a fine queen. Are you happy? You seem happy."

"I am very happy, Da'," I answered. "I never thought..."

"Aye," Da' chuckled. "I remember well the feeling of being able to claim your mate. I am only sorry this has happened now. If I could, I would lead the dragons myself but–"

"Da', I am your heir. We are not like others. We are dragons but you are king, and I am still learning to be. We cannot spend the day curled up with our mate, we have a duty to the clan. They are first. Our wants and desires are second. My mate knows this. She was the one who told me to go this morning."

"She is an amazing woman," Da' remarked.

"Aye, she is that," I replied wistfully. Da' chuckled.

"Then go back to her, lad. Tell her what you are doing and end this quickly so you can return to her."

"I intend to," I answered.

"Your report to me can wait. So long as nothing pressing happens, when you return, go to your wife."

"I thank you, Da'," I said. Bowing, I left the room in search of my wife.

Chapter Twenty-Nine

Brigid

Tahra and I walked through the bailey and out the side garden towards the ocean. Both our guards walking a safe distance behind us. As the keep was built into a mountain, the sides and front were the only ways in or out. But when Tahra turned and walked toward a rock face, I saw the façade. Two cuts were made along the mountain face, creating an illusion that there was no opening when there was a narrow passageway. Lir and I followed and soon we stood on the banks of the ocean, the keep behind us. Stairs led up to the back door, and our guards made their way up the steps, giving us privacy but watching everything. Gazing across the blue-black water, I took a deep breath. The image took my breath away.

"Oh, Tahra, it's lovely," I sighed. "How fortunate for you to grow up here with this beautiful view."

"Och aye," Tahra replied having crouched down to pet

Lir. "It was a good childhood. I hated how my brothers always teased me, though."

"Aye, brothers are meant to be like that. But thank your lucky stars you have them and your parents. I never had any siblings."

"Sometimes I wonder what that would have been like."

"Lonely," I replied softly. Tahra looked up at me as she rubbed Lir's belly.

"No need to be lonely anymore," she said standing and coming over to me. Taking my hands, she smiled. "You have us. And I have always wanted a sister. Sybine is nice but with the rivalry between my two brothers for her, I almost feel like she is theirs and I can't have her as a sister."

"That will not happen with me, Tahra," I answered. "I would be happy to be your sister." We embraced each other, but when Tahra pulled back, she had a question in her eyes. "Ask me," I prompted.

"Do you love my brother?" she asked.

I smiled softly. "Aye, very much."

She huffed and her brows furrowed.

"What is it?" I asked.

"How do you know?"

"Know what?"

"Know you love someone?"

"Oh," the question caught me off guard. "Well, I am not sure, honestly. I am new to love. But how I feel for your brother is he is almost a life source for me. Without him, I find I constantly think about him. His welfare is important to me. I love to make him smile and laugh and yet, I enjoy his possessive side too."

"That's his dragon," she explained.

"Aye, but his human part as well," I replied. "When he is

in danger, I fear for him. I find he means more to me than my own life. I would die for him if it meant he lived."

"Even if you are carrying his whelp? I think he would want you to live so there is something of him in the world."

"You are wise for one so young," I said. "Is there someone you had in mind when you asked me that?"

She looked down and concentrated on Lir. Finding a stick beside her, she stood and threw the branch along the bank for my deerhound to fetch.

"Perhaps," she answered.

I watched the young woman beside me. The sunlight caught her strawberry blonde hair and the wind whipped around her face. She had her father's brown eyes but her mother's and Finn's mouth and nose. She was beautiful.

"I want you to know, Tahra, I wish to be your friend. You may confide in me. I will tell no one," I said.

She looked down and took the stick back from Lir as he came bounding up. Throwing it again, she eventually spoke.

"I think, I have feelings towards someone," she admitted. "But I am nae certain."

"And these feelings, can you describe them?" I asked.

"A sort of giddiness when he's around. When in a crowd, I find myself seeking him out, wanting to be around him. But when I am, I am nervous I will say the wrong thing and will look a fool in his eyes. If he is hurt, it breaks my heart. When he touches my hand, I feel a sort of fire, akin to dragon's breath. I am sometimes ashamed of my physical response to him. Mama tells me it is natural but with dragon's sense of smell, I worry everyone knows of my... passion. That and, I see his dragon behind his eyes."

I paused. "What do you mean, see his dragon behind his eyes?"

"It is a legend. One I never thought of much before, until

recently. It is said if a dragon is another dragon's true mate, then they will see the dragon behind the eyes. It is a sign to let us know who we are meant to be with. Mama says she can see Papa's dragon, sometimes pacing, other times sitting or even sleeping, and he can see hers. I thought it was silly. Our dragons are us, and we are our dragons. How can someone see the image of one behind the eyes? But then, I saw Kai's. You've gone quite pale. Are you well?"

"Forgive me, I had not heard of the legend."

She observed me. "You saw Finn's, didn't you?" I nodded. "Oh, I am so happy!" she squealed and pulled me into a hug.

"As I am for you, Tahra. Kai is an excellent choice, I must say," I smiled. "So handsome, and such a great warrior and friend to your brother. I am pleased you like someone of his caliber. I am sure your parents would be happy with your choice as well."

"Do you truly think so?" she asked. "I know Finn and my other brothers tease me about my future mate but I donnae want them to scare Kai away."

"If he is scared away because of them, he is not the man I thought he was," I replied. "And donnae be surprised if they already ken. Do you have any indication if he cares for you the way you care for him?"

"Aye," she answered. "I sometimes catch him watching me and when I look at him, he just smiles slightly and looks away. He always escorts me even though it is not his position. And at the festival yesterday, with Mama's and Papa's permission, he was my escort which was a sign to all in the clan we are interested in each other. It is considered the first step to courting. Due to being the princess, I had to ask him. I was so nervous."

"I know the feeling," I stated.

"He said he wanted to but needed to ask the king's permission... I ken I am younger than he is but..."

"Your brother is older than I am. You are nearly twenty, he is only seven years older than you. It is not that much. Your brother is nine years older than me."

"I am needing to find a mate," she said. "All dragonwomen of childbearing age are expected to be married. I have reached that age a few years ago. A friend of mine is to be married to a dragonman in our clan soon. She is eighteen, a year younger than I. Up until recently War Chief was traditionally an unmateable position."

"Why?"

"Because of the danger and the time commitment. Papa struck that down after his father's War Chief stepped down and Kai took the position. I know about duty. I am a princess. I know he would be in danger and I know there would be nights he would not come to our bed because of his guard duty or council with Finn or Papa. But I donnae care. I have always learned that. Even as a young child, I understood duty."

"My mother was sister to the Laird and married to the clan War Chief. He fell in battle," I admitted. Her eyes widened. "But she also understood duty, as do I. But when you can have love along with duty, as I have with Finn, it is a wonderful thing. I hope everything will turn out well for you and Kai. He was the first friend I made here. He is fiercely loyal to your family. I will do all I can to encourage you both and be sure Finn agrees."

"Aye, he is my concern. I donnae ken if he would approve."

"He may approve more than you ken."

"Brigid," I heard Finn's voice call from the top of the stairs. Turning, I smiled brightly at him. His eyes lit when he saw me and he trotted down the steps, but his eyes flashed to slits and he let out a roar, telling us to get down. I was shocked, but my father's training allowed me to think. Grabbing Tahra, I flung us both to the ground just in time. An arrow grazed my forearm and skidded to a stop on the rocky soil.

Finn roared again but this time, it was a dragon's roar.

The whoosh of air overhead made me look up to see Finn's green dragon fly over the water and then dive to a small island. The guards were on us before I could breath.

"Tahra!" it was Kai. He raced to us pushing past the guards and grabbing her. His eyes passed over my sister-by-marriage. "Are you all right?" he demanded.

"I am fine, Kai," she answered. He gently took her chin in his hand and moved her face so he could see a red scrape and bruise beginning to form on her cheek. Movement near us seemed to break his thoughts.

"My lady," he looked at me. One guard held my arm as I pressed on my wound. Blood seeped between my fingers.

"I am well," I said through clenched teeth. In truth, it hurt. "I need a strip of linen and some yarrow crushed made into a paste. I donnae believe it will need stitching." *Thank the gods.*

"Get what her ladyship needs," Kai ordered one of the guards. "And tell cook to bring hot water." The guard bowed and hurried away.

"What the devil is going on here?" Bearcbhan shouted, running down the stairs followed by Teyrnon and Cahal.

"Someone shot at Tahra and I," I answered. My hands shook with adrenaline, and my heart pounded. Looking back to the island, I saw Finn dive and blow out his white fire. Not knowing what had happened, I looked from one brother to the other. Cahal watched the fight with indifference. Kai took my arm, looking back at Tahra.

"Go to her," I said then turned to the other guard. "Please help me inside before I cannae think. The blood and pain have started to cause dizziness."

"My lady,' he said and wrapped and arm around me, guiding me.

Thankfully, I felt no poison, but I was beginning to see speckles in the corners of my vision. Perhaps it was worse than I realized.

We all hurried into the Great Hall to be greeted by servants rushing around the room, obeying Erina's orders. The queen hurried to us, followed by the king. Erina's eyes passed over her daughter. Seeing she was not hurt, she turned to me.

"Get her to the chair," she ordered my guard.

"Kai," I heard Edan. He motioned him over. I watched Kai reluctantly leave Tahra's side. I could not hear their conversation and Tahra knelt by my chair.

"I am well," I soothed her concern.

"My lady!" Sara shrieked and ran over to me. "What happened?"

"Sara, I need you to get some tea ready. In the desk in my old room is a bundle of herbs. Find the lavender and boil it over a low flame. Let it steep for several minutes then bring two cups for her highness and me."

"Aye," she replied and hurried to do my bidding.

"The healer is here, Brigid," Erina said. "She has your paste ready."

"Aye, thank you," I said.

"I have some experience treating humans, lass. You rest. I'll have this taken care of in no time," a foreign voice said. The old woman appeared in front of me.

"'Tis the truth, I am growing tired."

"Close your eyes," Erina said softly. "Finn will be here soon."

I nodded, thankful for her calming tone. I closed my eyes.

Unsure how long I sat there, conversation and people blurred. I heard a loud bang, then was pulled up from the chair, somewhat harshly, and rammed into a hard, male chest. Finn. I melted into him.

Chapter Thirty

Finn

I was watching my wife and my sister walking on the banks of the loch, talking and playing with Lir. I did not want to interrupt them, though I smiled at what my dragon sensitive hearing had heard my wife and sister say about me and my best friend, Kai. Though he was a randy male, he was a great friend and an even better warrior. His admission to me earlier about seeing Tahra's dragon gave me hope. My thoughts turned to my wife. She stood wrapped in my plaid colors, her red hair blew about her and made my chest ache with love. I could wait no longer to have her loving gaze on me.

"Brigid," I called. She turned to me and my heart stopped when a smile split her face. By the gods, she was beautiful. Trotting down the stairs, I wanted to kiss her, but before I could think or even breathe, I saw a glint of something across the water on the small island Cahal, Kai, and I used to use as our hideaway. My eyes flashed to my dragon's keen sight and I saw a man with a bow and an arrow notched. I yelled at Brigid to get down and roared when the arrow was loosed. Brigid did not cry out when it struck her arm, but the sight and scent of her blood drove my dragon mad. Someone had hurt our mate. He took over and shifted.

We cut powerfully through the air and soon we were at the little island. The man fell backwards, trying to fire another arrow up at me. Blowing out my white fire, I lit the surrounding areas. The man fought the flames and he hurried to the other side of the small spit of land. I saw his boat moored and swooping down, grabbed it in my talons. With one strong clench, the wood splintered, and the boat broke apart. The man looked up at me in horror. Just as I was about to lunge towards him, I heard my brothers' roar. They were on their way. Looking back at them, I snapped my teeth, telling them to stay back. He was mine to kill.

Bearcbhan's gold dragon clenched his talon telling me they understood. Cahal's black dragon blew out his red fire impatient for a fight while Teyrnon's orange dragon, hung back watching. The man held his arms over his head fending off my flames. When I looked down at him, all I saw was the crest on his armbands.

The sun surrounded by a belt.

Lewis.

My blood ran cold. Brigid's own clan tried to kill her. They not only stole five of our females, but they tried to kill mine. The Lewis must wish for death. This archer was not the laird, but a messenger. I felt the acid burning in my throat. Brigid's face flashed before me, with blood on her arm where this bastard's arrow had caught her and that was all I needed. Letting out a roar, I blew the fire out directly on the man. When it cleared, he was a pile of ash.

Ignoring my brothers, I beat my wings with all the power I had, back to the keep. I needed to see to my wife.

When I landed, I shifted and immediately headed up the back stairs. My father and Kai met me. Handing me a plaid, I quickly wrapped it around my waist.

"Finn," my father said.

"Not now," I gritted, my dragon still in control.

"Aodhfionn," the power in my father's voice made me stop. My dragon, though still roaring in my head to make sure our mate was well, stopped a moment in respect to the king. "Go to your lass, but after, you will meet with me in the solar. I need to know what you saw."

"What I saw?" I demanded, taking a step towards him, my eyes flashing to slits and back. "What I saw was my mate and sister narrowly dodging an arrow. What I saw, was a wee bastard trying to kill her. I'm sorry father, but there will be no scouting party now. Lewis has declared war and I will be leading the charge."

"It was a Lewis then?" my father asked calmly.

"Aye, but not anymore. He's ash, fodder for the trees."

My father nodded slowly. "Go to your wife. Meet with me later. Kai, I will speak with you now. We have plans to make."

"Aye, my king," he stated.

Without another word, I turned and threw open the keep doors. The women parted but all I saw was Brigid, eyes closed while the clan healer dressed and wrapped her arm. I said nothing as I strode through the main hall to her. Grasping her, perhaps a bit too roughly, I pulled her into my chest holding her tightly. When she melted into me, my dragon roared for me to take her away. I needed to be sure my wife was not hurt.

Lifting her in my arms, I carried her up the steps. She wrapped her arms around me and buried her face in the crook of my neck. I took the stairs two at a time until I got to our room. Kicking the door closed, I carried her to the bed, and sat her down. When I pulled back to look at her, she opened her eyes. She was tired.

"I am well," she stated. My heart clenched. I pulled down the furs of the bed. Once she was situated, I slid in beside her and took her in my arms. She curled up against me. Her body relaxed.

"I am sorry."

"I love you," she said. "I am well, I promise. Just tired."

I kissed her forehead. "Sleep."

"Is he dead? The archer?"

"Aye."

"Good," she snuggled into me and closed her eyes.

Brigid

My whole body ached when I woke. I was pressed to Finn's side in our bed. He softly rubbed his fingers up and down my back.

Moving slowly, Finn's fingers stopped, and he looked down.

"Brigid?" he asked softly.

"Mm," I moaned. My head pounded and my forearm throbbed. "What time is it?"

"Just after twilight."

I turned to look at him, our faces so close I could see his dragon pacing behind his eyes. "Are you all right?"

I nodded. "My arm hurts but I am well. Tahra?"

"She is fine. Kai is standing guard."

"You know she loves him, aye?" I said.

Finn nodded. "Aye, and he loves her."

"She says she can see his dragon behind his eyes."

"That is a rare gift," he replied.

"It means they are true mates, aye?"

"Aye, it does. They are meant to be together."

I nodded. "I can see your dragon behind your eyes, Finn." He stared at me. "Are you all right with that?"

Pulling me into his chest he wrapped his arms around me and kissed me.

"Och, aye," he said pulling back. "I love you, Brigid."

"I love you, Finn, so very much," tears gathered in my eyes and trailed down my cheeks to his chest. "I never thought I would feel the sort of love I always wanted. And then I met you. I think part of me has loved you since I first saw your green dragon land beside me, and you stole me away."

"I have loved you since you rammed your wee dagger into my shoulder in the cave, he grinned, swiping his thumb beneath my eyes.

"Love me, Finn, please," I could think of nothing I wanted more than to have him make me his again.

"Och aye, love. I will love you well," he said.

Chapter Thirty-One

Finn

My father did not agree with my sentiment of a full attack on the Lewis clan. But as we worked together in his solar later that evening, planning what to do, he slowly came around to my idea of burning the keep.

"I won't have you burn it down," he said. "But a warning, aye, I agree."

"How many dragons will you spare?" I asked.

He crossed his arms over his chest and looked at the map we had out on the table between us.

"You command fifty, your brothers have twenty each, if you take yours and Bearcbhan's, I believe you would have plenty. All of you are to go with him." Da' looked at my brothers. "Send some scouts ahead and see where our females are."

"Already done," I said. "I did not think you would mind if I went about this quickly. While Brigid slept, I called for Kai. He took five others and they flew to the keep to see if our females were still alive."

"Normally, I would appreciate being consulted, but in this instance, time is of the essence. How you got Kai away from Tahra I'll never know."

"By using her to tell him to go."

Da' chuckled. "He's just as far gone as the rest of us."

"I'm still not sure about that union," Cahal grumbled.

"You aren't sure about any union, Brother," Teyrnon stated.

"Focus back," Da' said. "What did Kai see?"

"They are alive, but they have been stripped to their shifts and are standing out in the cold, chained together. When their guards fell asleep, one of the dragons landed and warmed them with his black fire. They will survive another few hours but, in this weather, we need to go quickly."

"I am grateful they are alive and glad Kai utilized Drake. Go now, lad. Rescue our females and be sure to report back to me. Be careful, all of you," Da' placed a hand on my arm. I nodded. My brothers left the room and Da' pulled me into an embrace, whispering in my ear. "I love you son and I am proud of you."

"Thank you, Da'," I said. Then, nodding, he released me, and we went out to the front of the keep. Mother, Brigid, Tahra, and Sybine waited for us. Mother embraced me and told me to be careful. My sister asked me to be safe and to watch over Kai. Then, I looked at my wife. She was so beautiful in the predawn light as she gazed into my eyes and smiled.

"Tell me what he is saying to you," she asked.

Pulling her into an embrace, I whispered. "He is telling me stay and make you mine again."

She laughed and hugged me tighter then pulled away, looking deep into my eyes. "Then tell him to do his duty well and return to me. I will reward him."

I groaned. "Love, believe me when I say that is his main goal, as it is mine."

"Then be careful," she replied. "I love you."

"I love you," I answered.

"Take care, dragonman," she kissed my cheek.

Winking, I took a step away from her and into the courtyard with the rest of the dragons. "We go to bring our females home!" I shouted. A cheer rang out and the warriors shifted. Throwing our long necks back, we each released fire, the rainbow of colors rising to the sky. Then we all beat our wings and jumped into the air. The sheer force of the wind made the women stumble back, but soon they caught themselves and watched us fly.

Stay focused, complete your duty, and get back to Brigid. I told my dragon. *No fighting, merely recusing our females.* Drake, the dragon with black fire, had told the females to prepare. When we freed them, they would need to shift quickly. I only hoped they were well enough to shift. They had not eaten, and the air was chilly. However, female dragons were hardy folk they would be well.

We met the six other dragons who still flew high above the keep, hidden in the clouds. Kai's blue dragon flew towards me giving me a signal. They were in position and ready. I nodded and spread my wings telling my warriors to prepare. I could not see our women. Looking over at Kai, he shook his head. Something was wrong. We both felt it. I looked back at my brothers. Cahal searched the skies. Bearcbhan watched below, Teyrnon observed the horizon. They all looked up at me. I did not trust Cahal. Motioning for him to stay back, Bearcbhan and Teyrnon moved forward. Fire flashing in Cahal's eyes but I ignored it and, once we were in position, I let out a roar and dived down to the bailey.

Chapter Thirty-Two

Brigid

Waiting was one of the hardest things imaginable. None of us knew how long it would be and no one was talking. The silence was deafening. Even the usual sound of the men training in the bailey was silent. We sat in the Great Hall, before the fire. The king paced, the queen and the three of us; Tahra, Sybine, and I, sat together.

Erina watched her husband then turned to us and forced a smile.

"Everything will be well," she said softly. "Now, how about we speak of something pleasant, hmm?"

I gripped Tahra's fingers, when I saw tears in her eyes. She was just as worried for her dragonman as I was for mine. Sybine sat stone-faced beside us. Bearcbhan had gone with them but so had Cahal, the two men, as I had been told, she loved. I knew little of the story, but it did not seem like the right time to ask.

"Perhaps," I started then cleared my throat. "Perhaps, we could talk about dragon traditions? I know little of them and am fascinated by them."

"Of course!" Erina said.

"Grand idea," Sybine breathed.

It was sometime later when we finally heard a dragon's roar, but everyone in the room tensed.

"What is it?" I asked, my stomach clenching. "What is wrong?"

"Someone is hurt," Edan muttered. The next second, he strode powerfully to the door. Erina, Sybine, Tahra, and I raced after him. We saw Bearcbhan's gold dragon, Kai's blue, Teyrnon's orange and another's red carrying a net with a large dragon inside. I searched the sky, but where Finn would normally be leading at the head, Cahal's black dragon led the group. I knew then, Finn had been hurt.

Letting out a scream, I raced from the keep.

"Brigid, get back!" Edan shouted. One of the other men, a tanner by his smell, grabbed me and moved me out of the way as the dragons landed. Cahal shifted first and started speaking.

"He is alive," he said. "But he is injured."

"What happened?" Edan demanded. The other men lowered the net gently and then shifted.

"We were searching for our women. The bastard had moved them, and Finn circled the keep. He landed on the spire and blew out his fire. When Kai signaled they had been found, Lewis came out of the keep and looked up, ordering the warriors to take him down. Finn let out a roar and dived at him. One of our women tripped and Lewis grabbed her. Finn had to pull up at the last second, but the archers were able to strike him. Lewis dropped the female and she scrambled away but too late. Finn had been struck."

"Finn," I screamed when the sides of the net fell away and I could see his beautiful green dragon. The hide was pale, and his eyes were closed. "Finn!"

I climbed over the net, not caring if the clan caught a glimpse of my underdress or bare legs.

"Where did they strike him?" I heard Edan ask.

"Shoulder. He couldn't fly and landed on his wing," Cahal explained. Erina covered her mouth but I heard her cry.

Seeing my dragon unconscious, I forced my fear away and allowed my healer training to take over.

"I need to be able to see the wound. Take him up to our room. I need hot water and bandages. Why hasn't his advanced healing helped him?" I questioned to myself.

"Donnae let him shift." Edan shouted. "If he shifts with a broken wing, he may never fly again. Call the healer, we must set the bones quickly."

I nodded once and turned to Kai and Finn's brothers. "How long does it take for bones to heal?"

"A day or so," Bearcbhan answered.

"Then hurry," I stated. The men nodded and shifted, taking Finn's net up to the balcony. I raced up the stairs and met them there.

Finn was still unconscious when he was lowered to our balcony. Fortunately, our room was large enough for several dragons to maneuver. They pulled Finn inside and shifted. Bearcbhan stepped forward.

"What can I do?" he asked.

"I first need to check him," I said scrubbing my hands in the water basin. "Can your sense of smell catch anything?"

"Smells like dragon bane," he answered. "A toxic but not fatal poison."

"What does it do?"

"It keeps dragons asleep and can force the dragon side to stay in control," Bearcbhan explained.

"Warn the dragon healer," I called. "I donnae ken how to handle dragon bane, but I can help him."

"I will stay and help you, mistress," the other dragonman offered.

"You have healer training?"

"My mother is the healer," he explained.

"What is your name?"

"Duncan."

"Duncan," I nodded. "Wash your hands and help me with the netting."

Three days and nights I waited. Waited for my husband, my lover, to wake. I held his massive dragon head in my lap, gently stroking his hard scales. Lir had curled up in the crook of my dragon's neck, his back to Finn's scales. After his initial whimpers when he saw his master injured, Lir had huffed a sigh and lay beside him, forbidding anyone other than me, Duncan, or the healer to come near. Finn's bones had knitted together well but the dragon bane kept him asleep.

On the fourth day, my body ached with fatigue and fear for my husband's safety. I held his head in my lap but slowly my eyes closed.

Chapter Thirty-Three

Finn

I woke from a dream as sweet as the finest honey. Brigid and I were in the groves near the waterfall where we had first spoken. Lir frolicked a ways away from us and we lounged together, making love on the soft grass. Taking a deep breath, I woke and opened my eyes. I was in dragon form. My dragon was still asleep, resting his head on Brigid's lap. But using his body like he used mine several weeks ago to speak with Brigid, I opened our eyes and gazed around the room. Another male's scent hit my nostrils and the possessiveness that coursed through me woke my dragon. He growled when he smelled the male.

Duncan came into our line of sight and it took everything I had to stop my dragon from flying at him.

"Rest easy, my prince," he said. "I am here to assist your mate. She could not do everything on her own."

I reasoned with my dragon that Duncan's mother was the clan healer and it was only right he help our mate, but my dragon would not be swayed. He perceived Duncan as a threat and when he lifted our head, I forced him back with all the strength I had. My eyes changed to human eyes and Duncan nodded.

"Your wing has healed, my prince," he said. "Shift if you have the energy."

My dragon roared his opposition, but I quelled him back and focused on shifting to my human form without hurting Brigid or waking her. If indeed it had been as long as it felt, she needed her rest. The pain of the shift made me want to shout, but I held it in. Once I was back in human form, Duncan came over to me and Lir looked up from my side.

"Hiya, lad," I breathed, and the deerhound licked my face, whimpering. "Shh, shh, I'm all right. Donnae wake your mistress." Lir nuzzled my neck and buried his face. Duncan knelt and eased his hand over my aching shoulder.

"Try not to move that too much, Finn," he said. "Your wing is healed but you will feel the pain in your human form now."

"Are the females well?" I asked.

"Aye," Duncan answered. "Slight bruising from where they were chained and some needed water and food, but they are well. I thank you for leading the charge. I could not imagine what my sister went through."

"Is she well?"

"Aye, thanks to your bravery. When I saw the fiend grab her and hold a knife to her throat... I wanted to kill him myself."

"Aye, I ken," I answered. "But all is well now. Is she with her mate and whelps?"

"She is and safe," he replied.

"How long has it been?"

"Four days, sire," Duncan answered. "Your bride has been by your side through it all. She only just fell asleep moments before you woke."

"She needs her rest," I replied.

"Aye and this beautiful creature guarded you fiercely only allowing my mother, myself, and your mate near you," Duncan said rubbing Lir's belly.

"He's a great warrior," I smiled.

"Do you think you can move?" Duncan asked after a pause. "I should help you to bed."

"I can, but I do not want to wake my wife."

"Then with your permission, I will carry her to your bed and return to help you. I will do naught but lay her down."

My dragon roared, no other male was to feel the weight of her body in his arms, but I knew rationally I could not carry her. Reluctantly nodding, I watched as Duncan eased Brigid back into his arms and smiled when I saw her frown and push away from him. She knew it was not my arms around her. True to his word, Duncan simply lay her down on the bed and turned away from her, to me. Assisting me up, we shuffled towards the bed and I lay down beside my wife.

"Sire, I would never dare presume, but knowing you were only recently mated, I caution you," he said. "You both need your *rest*." He stressed the last word.

"You mean do not take my wife to bed," I offered.

"You need to keep off that arm," he said.

"There are other ways, lad," I replied. The young male's cheeks turned pink and he looked away. "But I understand your concern and I thank you for it. I will be sure to fend off my wife's advances."

Duncan said no more as he helped pull the furs up around our bodies. Turning Brigid, I held her close to my side, her head resting on my good shoulder. Even in her sleep, she turned and threw one leg over mine and held me close. Lir padded over to us and lay down on the floor. Wrapping my arms around my wife, I slowly drifted off to sleep.

Brigid

I had fallen asleep! I could not believe it! *Finn, where is my dragonman? Is he well?* Had Duncan taken care of him? I tried to force myself awake but my body protested and would not budge.

"Shh, my love," I heard someone say. "All is well. Rest."

With those comforting words in my ear, I allowed my fatigue to overtake me again and fell into a deep sleep.

When next I opened my eyes, it was because something shifted under my head.

"Easy, my prince," Duncan's voice was near my ear, but it was Finn's groan that had my head raising before my eyes even opened.

"Finn?" I cried and looked down to see my husband's human form lying beside me.

"Good morning," Finn said.

I could say nothing as tears formed in my eyes and a lump in my throat. I threw my arms around his neck and held tightly. I did not know how tightly until I heard him groan.

"My lady," Duncan cautioned. "He is not fully healed." Pulling back far too quickly, my head collided with Duncan's nose.

"Oh Duncan, I'm so sorry," I cried. He held up the hand not clutching his bleeding nose and waved it off.

"Nay, 'tis all right," he replied. "I am well. I will tend to this and leave you be. I am glad you have awakened, my prince, my lady." He bowed out of the room and closed the door. Finn's chest bounced as he chuckled.

"I have nae seen Duncan retreat from a female's room so quickly before," he teased.

"I feel terrible," I said.

"Och, aye, but he is well," Finn replied. "I didn't hear a bone break."

We looked at each other for a time and after a moment, he cupped my face, pulled me down to him and kissed me. But our reunion was cut short by a knock on the door. I pulled away from him and hurried to the door. Opening it, Edan stood before me.

"May I have a moment?" He asked. "Duncan said he was awake."

"Of course," I replied and opened the door wider. The king stepped over the threshold and his eyes fell on his son, still in bed.

"Da'," Finn tried to sit up but flinched. I rushed to him.

"Donnae get up," Edan raised a hand to him. "I merely wanted to speak with you."

"Of course," Finn answered. "My love, could you give us a moment?"

"I will find Erina," I said. "If you have need of me..."

"I will call for you," he promised and, curtseying to Edan, I left them alone going in search of Erina and Tahra.

Chapter Thirty-Four

Finn

"Oh Finn, I am so glad you are all right," Da' said as soon as the door was closed behind Brigid.

"What happened after I arrived, Da'?" I asked.

"When we heard Cahal's roar we knew you were injured. Your brothers have asked after you when Duncan was seen. He stayed here with Brigid to assist her. The poor lass never left your side."

"She seems tired."

"Aye, she's a strong one." We were quiet for a moment, then Da' sat beside me. "What happened?" He asked.

"I am not absolutely certain," I admitted. "But it seemed the laird knew we were coming. Almost as if he was warned."

"I do not believe any of our clan would have warned him.

Especially not those you sent ahead as scouts."

"Have you spoken to the females? Could one of them have accidentally said something after Drake helped?" I asked.

"I have spoken with them. No one said anything."

"It was strange. They were moved and it was almost as if..." I trailed off.

"What, son?"

"Well, almost as if they had prior knowledge of when and how we would attack. I hate to say this Da' but I think someone told them."

"Who?"

"I donnae ken. And I have nae proof, but it was too much of a coincidence."

"We will keep our eyes and ears open. I'll speak with your brothers, too," he promised. I lowered my eyes and my father paused a moment. "You donnae think any of them had anything to do with this, do you?"

"Nay," I hurried to say. "I donnae *want* to believe it but... Cahal was part of the scouting pack. What if..."

"Och nay!" My father dismissed. "I donnae believe it. He may be a rash lad, but this? This is treason."

"Against me, Da', no' you. It makes some sense if he was trying to get rid of me."

"Nay. I donnae agree. He was worried about you. I will speak with Kai and see if he saw anything strange. Until then, let us keep this our secret."

"Aye. I will say nothing."

"Not even to Brigid. I don't want her involved," he ordered.

"Understood," I agreed. "I want to know why Lewis took our females and why he had Brigid attacked on our land. And could it have anything to do with the raid on our southern border. Something is deeper in this, Da'. I feel it."

"We need to wait it out. I will tell you what Kai says," my father stood and headed for the door.

"Thank you. Could you send Mum and Tahra in? I'm sure they are worried."

"They are but I needed to speak with you first. I will send them in. And tell your lass you need her."

"Allow her time with the others. She needs fresh air and time to herself. She's been as fierce as any mate."

"Aye, that she has. I'll tell her in a moment then."

"I thank you. Oh, Da'? I love you. I don't tell often you enough but when I felt the sting of the wound all I wanted was to say I love my family once more. My mate, my father and mother. My sister. And aye, even my brothers," I admitted.

"We love you too, Finn. I love you too. You have always made me proud. But now, rest. We will talk when you're better."

Brigid

Finn was well enough to join the others for dinner that evening. As we entered the main hall, a chorus of cheers rang out. Finn smiled and thank our clan for their support. Walking up to the dais where our family stood waiting for him, I fussed over him, making sure he was well. Taking my hand in his, he squeezed and had me sit beside him.

"Glad to see you well, brother," Teyrnon said slapping him on the back. Finn winced, and I glared at my brother-by-marriage. "Oops, sorry, I ken better than to offend a female."

"Just a little tender," Finn answered rolling his shoulder.

"We are glad to see you here, love," Erina said.

"I am glad to be here, Mum. Where is Cahal?" Finn looked over at his father and an unknown look passed between them.

"He decided not to join us. We have not seen him for a day or so," Edan said.

"Probably slaking his battle induced lust with some willing human female in the nearby village," Teyrnon said.

"Teyrnon!" Edan snapped. "There are ladies present. Not to mention, they are your mother and sisters. Watch yourself."

"I meant no disrespect, Da' but when he left the scouting party before Finn and Bearcbhan arrived we did nae ken where he went. He claims he had a female waiting for him. But I'm not sure it's true. He had no scent on him afterwards."

Finn looked over at his father again but Edan didn't react.

"He is troubled, that one," Edan replied. "I'm sure he was seeking some time to himself."

"Perhaps you can speak to him, love," Erina said to her husband.

"If he shows, I will," Edan promised. "Until then," he raised his wine goblet. "Let us celebrate our son's health."

Chapter Thirty-Five

Finn

Two months later

She was sick. She didn't think I noticed, but every morning she dragged herself out of our bed to vomit in the chamber pot. I had been able to keep my dragon under control, telling him it had to be something she ate. But on the seventh day, I could not hold him any longer. My dragon burst forward, leapt out of bed, and raced to our mate.

I could do nothing as he bellowed for the healer. He kept me tightly reigned in.

"'Tis nothing, my love. I assure you, I am well," she said.

"You have been sick for days, Brigid. It is *not* nothing. And you will be looked at," my dragon ordered.

"Do not try and assert your power over me, Dragon. Now give me back Finn," she replied.

"He will not protect you like I can." I growled at my dragon.

"I want my husband," she said deliberately.

"We are one in the same," he grumbled.

"Fine," she huffed. "Give me the other one of you."

I pushed against his hold, telling him she needed me, not the rough dragon. Finally, my beast gave way and I took control.

"Are you well?" I asked. "You have been sick. Should I have the healer come?"

"Nay, my love. I merely wanted you," she threw her arms around me and I held her close.

"Nae matter what it is, we will go through this together," I encouraged with far more confidence than I felt.

"I know," she replied. "I think I know what it is."

"Donnae say anything yet. Let the healer look at you."

"Finn!" Kai banged on the door.

"What?" I bellowed back.

He tried the door, but it was barred. Looking down at Brigid, she nodded, and I let her go. Sinking down onto our bed, she looked awfully pale. But I could think no more on it. I opened the door to see my best friend standing there.

"What?" I demanded again.

"You must come now," Kai replied, and I could see the tension in his eyes.

"What happened?"

"It's the twins," was all he said. My heart stopped momentarily. My nephews. Wee bairns.

"Oh god," I looked back at my wife, her eyes wide with terror. She hurried to the chair beside the fire and pulled my plaid around her shoulders.

Together we rushed out of the room, down the stairs and out the back where Tahra and Brigid walked not two months ago.

A small crowd had formed, circling something on the ground. *Dear god, please let them be alive*, I thought.

"What happened here?" I demanded pushing through the crowd.

Finally, I looked down to see my sweet baby nephews bloody and beaten but alive. Falling to my knees, I cradled them on my arms, my wife kneeling beside me.

"Where is Bearcbhan?" I yelled hopeful he hadn't done something stupid.

"What's going on?" I heard his voice. Giving my nephew to my wife, I stood and blocked my brother. Dragons were very protective of their young and seeing his sons, his first-born sons like that, would cause his inner dragon to take over and demand revenge. But I was too late. Screaming their names, he fell to his knees and cradled them to his chest. Sybine rushed to the scene and knelt beside her husband.

"Who did this?" I demanded.

Several dragons looked down, but a couple looked at my wife with murder in their eyes. That told me all I needed to know. Lewis. Brigid locked eyes with me. She knew too.

Dragons began shouting at once, the clatter too much for me to think. My father's bellow shook the pebbles on the beach.

"Anyone who has knowledge of this, step forward," he ordered.

Two sentries stepped forward. "We saw the young princes playing one moment, then the next, they were ambushed. Before we could get to them, they were as you see. Cullum went after them. He caught one but he turned his dagger on himself before he could apprehend him. But my king, he wore the Lewis crest."

The air around us shifted and I could feel the hair on the back of my neck stand on end. Looking around the group, all eyes were on my mate. Glancing up at my father, his almost imperceptible nod was enough for me. I bent down to whisper in Brigid's ear.

"We must go."

"I cannae. They need me," she said.

"I love you for wanting to take care of them, but we have to leave, now. Come with me," I pressed.

She turned her gaze up to me and must have seen my dragon pacing behind my eyes because she nodded and slowly rose. Taking my hand, she gave me her trust. I walked her away from the fray and to an open area. The eyes of my clan followed us and though my dragon watched them warily, we both knew we had to get her away. I shifted as quickly as I could and lifted her up to ride on my back. Seeing several clansmen start to shift as well, I jumped into the air and beat my wings as fast as I could to get her away from what I knew was coming.

Brigid

Finn took off so quickly I thought I was going to be sick. My stomach roiled and I was sure it was not only because of the child I carried. I had yet to tell him of my suspicions, but I was nearly certain I carried his child. As bile rose in my throat, I tried to prevent my sickness, but it was of little use. Vomiting, I made sure to turn my head away from Finn's dragon, but I knew he felt and heard me. The muscles in his back stiffened. Turning his head around to look at me, his eyes changed to human and questioned if I was all right. Nodding, I tried to put him at ease, but my heart hurt. Our clan knew I was a Lewis, probably thought I was a spy, and they turned against me. Granted they were only protecting their own, but I would never hurt a child. Placing my hand on my stomach where I hoped life grew, I swore I would never allow a child to be hurt.

Just as I lowered my chest to my husband's neck and held on, giving him a hug, I heard him roar and then bank to the left, but I felt the hot sear of my flesh tearing on my shin. Looking down, my blood dripped along with Finn's. His shoulder had been torn, but he kept flying. Knowing he would be worried when he smelled my blood, I tore a piece of my chemise and with more grace than I expected, I tied the fabric around the wound. It was a scratch, but it burned. Finn's wings faltered for a moment and I looked down. The gaping wound was draining him. He needed to land and let his accelerated dragon healing work. Scanning the horizon, I pointed out the cave he had taken me to the first day we met. He nodded and headed that way.

Finn

Blinking my eyes hard, trying to clear them of the dark spots in the peripheral, I glided down to the flat entry of the cave. Whatever I was shot with was causing me to lose focus. Landing with a little difficulty, I hoped my wife was well. I felt her vomit earlier and I knew she was still not used to me taking off so quickly.

Brigid stumbled but caught herself and turned to look at me. My dragon collapsed and breathed heavily. We were both exhausted.

She rushed to me and only then did I see her limping and the linen wrapped around her leg. I looked sharply up at her, my eyes questioning.

"I am well," she said. "Are you?"

My dragon wanted to curl up and lick his wound, but I couldn't let that happen. Brigid needed me. Pushing to the front of my mind, I took over and shifted back to my human form with an agonizing roar. My shoulder ached horribly.

"Are you all right?" I pleaded.

"Me? I'm not the one with the gash in his shoulder," she

replied.

"Brigid tell me." My hands went over her body taking her in, making sure she was all right.

When my hands went to her abdomen, I froze. There was a small knot beneath the folds of her gown. My dragon took notice. I didn't realize I knelt before her until her hands came into my hair. I was fascinated by the small bundle not knowing what it meant.

Leaning forward at my dragon's urging, I took a deep sniff, smelling her scent all the way into the marrow of my bones but then it hit me. My scent as well. My essence. My child. I snapped my head up to look at her, begging confirmation from her blue eyes.

She nodded. "I wanted to tell you. But then everything else happened. You're going to be a father."

Love, protection, strength, and virility flooded my veins making me heady. Standing faster than I should have, I grabbed her to me and kissed her until I could hardly breathe.

She carried my son. My heir. My child.

The thought of being a father made my heart swell. The thought of Brigid being the mother of my children made me melt, so much so I didn't hear the intruders until it was too late. I felt a pain in my back, and fell to the ground, my vision clouding. I could hear Brigid scream my name as three men grabbed her, including the traitorous bastard who had tricked her the first time. I couldn't move. My dragon roared at me to protect our mate, our child, but my body wouldn't react. I saw them dragging her out, my lass was fighting them, but they were too strong. Finally, one of them bent down to me and sneered.

"You want your witch back?" He taunted. "Bring the keys to the treasury and we won't burn her like the witch she is. You have one day."

Her scream haunted me as everything faded to black.

Chapter Thirty-Six

I woke at my father's urging. Duncan was beside me, laying strips of something foul smelling on my shoulder and side. The bastards had struck me from behind.

"Where is Brigid?" I demanded sitting up quickly. I was in my bedchamber. "Where is she?"

"I do not know," my father replied. "She was not in the cave when I found you. I could scent others, but I didn't see your lass."

"They took her," I answered. "I must go after her. Dear gods, they will burn her. How long has it been?"

"Only an hour. I followed you when I knew it was safe. Bearcbhan was inconsolable. The twins are healing well but I am worried he will try something on his own."

"They want me to bring the keys to the treasury. You ken, as I do, being your heir, I am the only one with them. They want the treasure and they will kill my wife to get it," I confessed.

"Aye, I feared as much when you told me about the silent raid on our south border. That door would lead them straight to the treasury. We cannot give them the keys, but we can save your lass," my father stated.

"She will not be welcome here any longer. You saw the looks they gave her. Perhaps it is time I step down. My brothers have wanted my title for a long time, and I will not give up my wife nor my child."

"Your child?" He questioned.

"Aye, Brigid carries my whelp."

My father leaned back with a surprised look on his face, but a soft smile grew. "I am happy for you, lad but I will not have you abdicate. You are my rightful heir."

"I will not give up my mate nor have her fear for her safety."

"If I may," Duncan spoke up. "Forgive me for speaking out of turn, my king, my prince. But I hear things. The people love their princess. They were angry our young were injured but they would die for their future queen. The anger you sensed was not directed at her specifically. Merely the bloodline that forced her into this. Aye, we all kenned she was not willing at first. But we love her as you do. She is our future queen."

"Thank you, Duncan," My father spoke. "Perhaps you could leave us for a moment?"

"Aye, of course," he said. "You will heal soon my prince."

Once we were alone, I turned to my father. "Where is Cahal?"

My father looked down. "I donnae ken. He was not in the keep when we called for him."

Instead of anger at my brother's betrayal, I felt only pain. The pain of my own blood betraying my confidence, my hope, and my love.

"I need to go after my wife. They will kill her."

"Aye, and we will, lad. But the time has come for a full attack. What they have done, will not stand. But we must do so with patience."

"My lord!" Frantic pounding on the other side of the door jarred us both. Sybine was banging on the oak. "My lord, please! Help!"

My father jumped up and raced to the door. Once open, Sybine fell into his arms weeping. My mother stood behind her; her expression grim.

"What the devil?" My father cursed.

"It's Bearcbhan," my mother said calmly. "He's gone after Lewis on his own."

"He was so angry. The healer is worried about the lads' dragons. He lost his mind. His dragon took over. I begged him to stop, but he didn't. He flew. I'm so worried. He is not in his right mind. Please help him!" Sybine begged.

My father turned to me and I nodded. Having sensed my own child, I understood his pain.

"We fly. Now," he stated.

Chapter Thirty-Seven

Brigid

I was thrown to the ground before my uncle, seeing the sick grin of satisfaction on his face. His wife stood silently beside him, no longer pregnant. I prayed for her sake she had a boy. He would make no more designs on her if she did. A fate I am sure she would appreciate. His young son from his first marriage, stood on his other side, already looking far too much like the ugly tyrant before me.

"So," my uncle began. "You have come back."

"I never came back. Your men abducted me. Take me back to my clan immediately. I demand it."

"You demand?" He chuckled, though there was no mirth behind it. "I see you have not learned your place, witch."

"I am Brigid MacKay, wife of Aodhfionn MacKay, heir to the throne and lairdship of the MacKay. First born of the king and champion of all dragon warriors. You will let me go back to my people or they will descend upon you with dragon fire and death."

For a moment, the laird paused. The people cowered and huddled together, but soon my uncle's cool exterior settled back as a mask on his withered face.

"Tie her to the stake. If her husband refused to bring us the keys we need, then he will see his wife's chard remains on his doorstep," he ordered.

"You do not know my husband," surprised by my own confidence, I stared him down, but his men grabbed me.

I did not fight them. I knew it was fruitless, but I prayed harder than I ever prayed before to see my husband's green dragon form circle in the sky.

Hold tight, little one. I soothed my child. *Your father will save us.*

The ropes were secure, my arms above my head, my legs tied at the knees. Bile rose to the back of my throat. I had faith Finn would save me, save us, in time. But as the sun sunk behind the trees, I began to fear. I had not seen his wound and wasn't sure of his fate. Suddenly, I heard it. The sound of beating wings. My heart soared and my eyes searched the sky. Though no green dragon descended, instead, a black one landed with a mighty quake.

Cahal.

"Where have you been?" My uncle demanded. "You were supposed to speak with me ages ago." Cahal whipped his head around to glare at my uncle. "I am not accustomed to be kept waiting."

Raising his head, the black dragon blew out fire, a deep orange... not Cahal's red color. The dragon shook his body and black tar flew on to the spectators. I could not believe my eyes.

He shifted.

"You do not dictate when I am to speak with you. Remember your place, human," the voice said.

"I am laird," my uncle argued.

"And once you kill my brother and his witch, I will be king. So, watch the tongue in your head or I'll carve it out."

"Teyrnon!" I gasped. He turned to look at me, all form of mirth gone from his eyes. In its place was ice, cold as iron. "Why?" I breathed.

He chuckled but did not answer my question. "I told you to wait a little while longer." He spoke to my uncle. "We do not know if she is carrying his whelp. It would make the pain that much more intense."

"I care not for your perverted sense of revenge. I want what's mine," my uncle said.

"And you will get it. Half of the treasure, as agreed," he assured. My heart clenched. The whole time we all thought it was Cahal who betrayed us... but no.

"I want more than that," my uncle complained.

Teyrnon's nostrils flared, and I saw smoke tendrils seep out. "That is what we agreed. Half. No more, no less."

"It's not enough. What have you done? Nothing. I have done everything. I gave you the witch when you told me your plan. I took her back. What have you done?" My uncle demanded.

"I have given you everything you want. It was my plan. My ideas that brought us here. Who warned you about the attack? Who told you of the secret passage in the south country? Who led your men to it? Who snuck them in? Who called off the guards so your men could take females? It was me. I gained their trust. They blame Cahal and once Finn and Brigid are dead, I will tell my father what we agreed and Cahal will be slapped in irons. I will be king. Do not forget to whom you speak, human."

Just then there was a loud roar and I looked up. Cahal's black dragon dived out of the sky, barreling toward his brother. Teyrnon roared and quickly shifted. Jumping out of the way, Teyrnon leapt into the air and high above us, they fought.

Then, I heard it. A loud dragon roar.

"What was that?" My uncle demanded, looking up.

"That," I drew his attention. "Is my husband."

Just as I spoke those words, Finn's green dragon descended behind me with a mighty crash. His tail whipped around me, shielding me from those around us. He let out another loud roar and the echoing dragon responses, took my breath away. They had come. I caught Finn's eye and nodded. I was well and he needed to know that. The rest of the dragons descended. My uncle's warriors were no match. But I did not care. Finn cut my bonds and I threw my arms around him.

"I knew you would come for me."

Finn helped me up to ride his neck as usual but before he could fly, "Brigid!" I heard a woman scream. I looked over to see my uncle's wife fighting her way to me. "Brigid! Please! Take me with you!"

Finn growled.

"No wait," I said to him. He looked up at me. "She is a victim, like me and everyone else affected by my uncle. And she's a friend. Please."

Finn stared at me, then his eyes changed to human and he nodded.

"Hurry, Cairstine," I shouted. She rushed to us and Finn offered his talon. Without a moment's hesitation, she climbed up and held on. She was in a horrible situation with my uncle. Still, it surprised me how she carelessly climbed into a dragon's talon. Once she was situated, I leaned down and spoke in Finn's ear.

"Fly, Finn," I said. He beat his wings and jumped into the air.

Chapter Thirty-Eight

Finn

Seeing Brigid tied to the stake was more than I could bear, but at my father's command, I waited. We arrived just as Cahal and Teyrnon flew at each other. Seeing my brothers fight made me ache to jump in and help Teyrnon. That traitorous Cahal was no match against two brothers.

Finally, when my father gave the signal I roared and dived to protect my mate. Landing beside her, I whipped my dragon tail around her, protecting her from the humans. As agreed, I paid little heed to the fight around us, I merely cut through the ties that bound her and felt her throw her arms over me.

"I knew you'd come for me," she said. My dragon and I puffed out our chest at our mate's trust. We would always be there for her and our whelps.

Carrying both humans to the encampment, we were just to the tree line when I saw Bearcbhan's form racing into the fray. He was in no state of mind to fight and though I tried to stop him, he barreled past me to the Lewis laird. Cahal turned to look at him. Bearcbhan was no match for him. Cahal flew toward him with all his strength, almost possessed.

I had to help. Landing, I set Brigid and the other human down. She nodded quickly and I raced back to the fight. Turning my attention to my brothers, Cahal had nearly reached Bearcbhan. But then, to my absolute horror and shame as I didn't see it before, Teyrnon's dragon flew beneath Cahal's and interceded. His and Bearcbhan's dragons rammed into each other and Teyrnon bit into Bearcbhan's neck with no remorse. Bearcbhan shrieked in pain and surprise, but I was too late to save him. Teyrnon ripped his throat out and Cahal roared. My gaze flew to my father who watched in agony as his youngest son plummeted to his death, landing with a thud. Everything froze as if time itself knew the severity of the situation.

My father's red dragon let out the most mournful wail I had ever heard. In that moment, his eyes blazed, and he flew at Teyrnon. Cahal then turned his attention to me. His eyes sorrowful as we both mourned our youngest brother. But then, his eyes moved over my shoulder and he roared. My head whipped around only to see that bastard, Kane running toward Brigid and the other human. Turning, I raced back, feeling Cahal close behind me.

All the times I thought he was the traitor, only to be so completely and utterly wrong, was a sobering thing. He was always in the shadows. I would need to speak with him. I remembered all the times he was there, seemingly out of nowhere. The one I remembered the most was when he landed on the balustrade on my wedding night. According to Brigid, he had not approached until he saw her walk out of our room. Could my father have been correct? Could he have been protecting us all along? Brigid specifically? And what was it he had said that day I challenged him? It was not just him there that night...

I had no time to think.

Cahal and I landed between Kane and Brigid. I faced my wife and picked them both up, carrying the humans away. With one final look at Cahal, he nodded at me and it was as if I had the old Cahal back. We always could read each other's minds. Turning to the bastard, Cahal toyed with Kane only a few moments before turning him to dust. I expected to hear a shriek from the laird's wife, but I heard nothing nor sensed any fear. She was a strong woman.

I let out a soft roar and Cahal looked over at me. I looked pointedly to the keep and Cahal nodded once. Lewis was mine.

Beating my massive wings as quickly as I could, I saw the small camp just beyond the trees in a glen. My mother greeted us and ushered Brigid and Cairstine away. My wife turned to me once before I hurried back to the fray.

Be careful. She mouthed and with a quick nod, I flew with all my might back to the Lewis keep.

It ended today.

Chapter Thirty-Nine

Finn

My dragon eyes scanned the battlefield for the Lewis Laird. The coward was skulking away from the fight, using five guards to shield him. Cutting off his retreat by blazing my white fire against the side of the keep, I landed before him. He screamed. The putrid smell of fear and soiled trousers reeked from his men's bodies as they stood before their laird, swords pointed at me, shaking. It was almost comical.

With a few flicks of my wrist they were thrown to the side, leaving just the laird and me. He looked up at me, a scared weakling. All I could see was the man who had made my wife's life a living hell. The man who had burned her mother, his own sister at the stake and who had ostracized my wife for fifteen years. The same man who sold her to me, though I was grateful for that. The same man who sent his man to try to kill her, who stole our females as they were washing clothes in the burn. The same man sent his soldiers to hurt my nephews and abduct my mate. He did not deserve mercy, but I wanted to kill him as a man.

Pushing to the forefront of my dragon's conscious, I requested the honor of killing him. My dragon grumbled but relented when I told him it would not be quick.

I transitioned into my human form and stood before the laird. Though my nakedness drew his attention with surprise and disgust, I used it for my advantage. Grabbing one of the swords from the ground, I leveled it at him. Cahal, back in human form, came up behind me, a plaid draped over his hips.

"Mercy," Lewis said.

"You wanted the keys to my clan's treasure?" I started, speaking to the laird. "You stole my wife to ransom her and hurt innocent children. You killed my brother and expect mercy?"

"I didn't kill him!" he protested. "It was Teyrnon. It was all Teyrnon's plan. I will tell you everything."

"Pick up the claymore and fight me as a man. Or are you too weak, old man?" I did not care about anything he and my traitorous brother had planned. Once the laird was dead the plan would be over.

The laird's eyes blazed at the insult I leveled. Had he been dragonborn, his nostrils would have smoked. He bent to pick up the sword. "'Tis not a fair fight," he began. "You have a champion behind you, I have no one."

"That is not my fault but if you so desire it... Cahal, should this feeble old man defeat me, you are to allow him to pass. I shall have your word on it."

"Aye, brother. You have my word," Cahal swore.

"Then let us begin," I said.

The laird made the quintessential mistake at the beginning of our sparing; he attacked in anger. His haphazard blows were childish and imperfect. I easily deflected his unpracticed strikes and toyed with him for a moment. He did get one strike I did not expect, and my forearm burned from the slight cut but by the time he regained his ground the wound had already started to heal.

The battle was waning fast and the dragons were victorious. Our losses were heavy on our hearts but as the laird parried once more, I had enough and only wanted to hold my wife to me. With a deft blow, I cut into the human, his blood spraying out of him. Falling to his knees, he looked up at me. His surprised eyes reflected my determined ones. One more strike and he fell dead at my feet. I wiped his blood from my face. My wife was avenged, my dragon was satisfied.

Pulling on the plaid I had in the pouch tied to my ankle, I turned to my brother. I was hesitant, before extending a hand to him. He accepted it in a warrior's shake and pulled me into an embrace.

"I am sorry for all this time, Brother," Cahal said. "I was angry and bitter at Bearcbhan's and Sybine's betrayal and took it out on my family. I am sorry. I overheard Teyrnon one evening bragging to a lass from the human village about his grand plan and I decided to wait and watch. He planned on killing Brigid. I tried to protect her when I could. I am only so sorry I could not reach Bearcbhan in time."

"He fought valiantly and was taken by surprise. We did not ken Teyrnon was the traitor," I tried to encourage him.

"You all thought it was me. Aye, I ken. But I assure you," he knelt and took out his dagger. "My only loyalty is to my king, my people, and my clan. You, as father, have my loyalty now and always."

Stunned by his actions, I did not speak until I heard our father behind me. "My lads," he called. "Are you well?" Only when I turned did he see Cahal on his knee pledging his loyalty to me. He nodded for me to continue and I placed a hand on my brother's right shoulder.

"I would be honored to have you at your rightful place,

by my side, Brother," I said to Cahal. He smiled up at me and for the first time in nearly five years, I had my best friend back.

My father came over and embraced us both.

"Brigid?" He asked.

"Safe with mother. Our losses?" I asked.

"We mourn three and two are gravely injured," he explained.

"Bearcbhan?" Cahal asked anxiously.

My father looked down and I saw him subtly wipe a tear. "One of the three we mourn."

"Nay," Cahal breathed. "I tried, Father. I tried to get to him."

"I ken you did, lad. I saw all. He was angry and did not see your brother's betrayal. He will be given the warrior's funeral he deserves, and we must all look after the twins and his daughter, as well as his mate."

"They will be as if mine," Cahal proclaimed.

"I am counting on it," my father said. "Now, we must get the wounded back home and bury the dead."

"Who is wounded?" I asked.

"Kai is amongst them," he explained.

"Nay," I worried over my best friend. Tahra would be devastated.

"Not serious but he is in for a long recovery. Come with me, lads. Help me with our dead," Da' said.

We turned with our father and made our way to our brother's body, no longer in his dragon form. At death, the dragon goes before the human and the human shifts back. Bearcbhan lay at the bottom of a ledge, his body broken, his throat ripped out. Tears pricked my eyes. I remembered when he was a boy, training, learning from both Cahal and me.

"Where is the nameless who did this?" I demanded. To be called *nameless* in our traditions was the greatest curse. I would not dishonor my mother by calling him something else.

"He is dead," my father stated without emotion. "And will always be a traitor to our clan. Nameless evermore. I will have nothing written about him. No tales nor songs. He is no son of mine."

Without another word, we lifted Bearcbhan's body and carried him back to the landing area in order to wrap him in cloths until we arrived back at our lands.

Leaving my father and brother, I went to our wounded. One warrior had a deep strike across his chest that had already begun to heal but the other wound against his neck worried me. The dragons trained in battlefield dressing, were already pressing clean linens to the wound. Kai lay next to him. His face pale and his eyes closed. It frightened me for a moment, until I took his hand and felt life pulse beneath the skin.

Good. Our sister would be most displeased if we allowed him to die, my dragon said.

Our sister is a child. Kai is a man in every sense of the word. And his tastes for women in the bedchamber border on extreme, I argued.

Still. She cares for him and I see a change in him whenever she is near. I ken you will give them a chance. You cannae lie to me. They would make gifted and beautiful young, my dragon replied.

I donnae desire to think of our sister making young with any man. Let us leave our friend be and pray he will recover, I let the conversation drop.

Returning to my father and brother, we assisted with the other two dead and got them into a basket.

"My lord! Wait, please!" A woman called. She carried a bundle in her arms. My father waited for her to come closer.

She stopped a short distance away and curtsied.

"Approach," my father ordered.

"My lord, I am Elspeth, Cara's sister," she said. My father motioned for her to continue. "My lord, I watched the battle from above, and I am only so glad you killed the laird. He was a tyrant as you ken. But his young bride flew, with him," she gestured to me. My father did and said nothing. "This," she motioned to the bundle in her arms. "Is her infant daughter. I beg of you; she needs her mother."

I saw my father take a deep breath. "And you?" he asked.

"I am the child's caretaker. We fall under you, my king. If you'll have us. Not all Lewis are disloyal and not all followed him. Please, I beg of you, donnae leave us vulnerable."

Da' sighed but looked around the small group. Then looked at me. He would be stepping down in five months, it would fall to me. I nodded.

"Those who desire to leave are able. We hold no prisoners and have taken our revenge. *If* you would like to join us or be closer to us, pack what you can and journey south. All who pledge loyalty will be welcome. Hear me though, any traitor or one coming to us for nefarious purpose will be swiftly and severely punished." Several humans agreed. My father took the infant and turned to look for a warrior.

Odalis, Cara's mate stepped forward, offering to take the babe.

"You," Da' called to a warrior I had seen turn sides earlier and fight for us. "What is your name?"

"I am Rhys, my king," he knelt.

"My son," Elspeth said.

"You fought for us, why?" Da' questioned.

"Because I have always honored my clan and the laird who led us dishonored the name of Lewis. I fought for a future. And my aunt always spoke well of you. And my uncle is one of you."

Odalis stepped forward. "If I may, my king," Da' nodded for him to continue. "I ken Rhys. He is Cara's nephew. When we have visited, I've spoken at length with him, trained him even, if I may claim that. He is not loyal to Lewis and would be an asset to us."

"Uncle Odalis stepped into my father's role when he was led to war and died by the laird's actions. I would pledge to you here and now," he placed a hand over his heart.

"Later, lad," Da' said. "Here is my first commission for you. You ken our lands?" the boy nodded. "Lead those you deem loyal to us. We accept all who desire it. Those you deem disloyal, do with as you will."

Without another word, my father turned to the rest of us and spoke.

"We shift and fly."

All dragons except Odalis, shifted. Carefully, the warrior stepped into one of the empty baskets with the babe tucked against him. Another dragon carefully clutched the top of the basket in its claws.

As one, we flew back to our females and the encampment.

Chapter Forty

Brigid

Crina heard the men coming before any of the rest of us did. Moving through the camp, she called for the women to bring hot water and linens for the wounded as well as ale for the hearty. She encouraged us to keep bright spirits, but I knew deep down she had felt the loss of her sons. Sybine and Cairstine sat beside me, stone faced as I brewed a tisane for those wounded internally, but I held Sybine's hand when she began to shake.

"I ken he has passed," she whispered softly. "I felt him leave me."

I said nothing. I knew it was true. Her body shook harder as she tried valiantly to hold back tears. "What will become of my whelps? Fatherless. And me? Without my mate?"

"They will be well looked after. They have uncles who

love them," I encouraged.

If possible, she went another shade paler and averted her eyes. "You must ken what happened between Cahal and myself," she started.

"That has naught to do with me, my dear. All I can say is he is a valiant warrior who helped save me."

"I left my child," Cairstine said mournfully. "I was so set on getting away. How could I have done that?"

"Fear not," I turned to her. "All will be well. I know it."

"Our males are here," Erina said to the group of women gathered. All eyes turned up to the skies. I recognized Finn's green dragon flying to the right of a massive red one. Obviously, the king. Cahal's black dragon flew to his father's left and the others behind. I searched the skies for Teyrnon in chains but could not see him. A few dragons carried baskets but Edan carried one specific one and Sybine burst into tears. I put my arm around her as Erina held Tahra close as she wept.

With great love and respect, Edan laid the bundle down and landed beside it. Locking eyes with his wife for a moment, he lowered his head.

A moment of silence stretched but then Edan reared his head back and let out a mournful roar. The dragons beside him did the same but the women stayed silent as they mourned their clansmen and family.

Edan shifted back to his human form and wrapped a kilt around his hips. Finn and Cahal did the same but when Finn caught my eye, he shook his head for a moment. I could not go to him yet. There was something he needed to do first.

Edan stepped forward and spoke to Sybine.

"He fought valiantly. A true dragon warrior. I am honored to have called him my son. He died a hero. We will look after you and the bairns," he said.

Sybine wept but looked up at her father-by-marriage. "I

have the right to know his killer and pass judgment on him."

"He has already met his maker," Edan snarled, angry at the situation, not at her request.

"Still," she pressed. "Who was it?"

Edan lowered his head again and announced; "we had a traitor in our midst. It will be to my ever shame I did not notice it sooner. This is the last time I will say or hear his name. From now on, he will be nameless... Teyrnon betrayed us all." The gathered dragons gasped, and murmurs rose around us. "Your prince, my son Cahal, learned of the plot and tried to stop it. He protected your future queen and kept a close eye on The Nameless, who wanted the crown for himself. The Nameless partnered with the Lewis Laird, bartering our treasure for his help destroying our clan. He set his sights on the crown and was willing to kill his own family for it. I am who you should pass judgment on, Sybine. For it was my folly that allowed his to go unchecked."

Those gathered were quiet as Sybine stared at Edan. "You have always treated me as your daughter, my king. I could never judge you. His folly is his alone."

Edan looked up at her and nodded. Reaching forward, he offered his hand to her. She raced into his arms and wept. Edan looked back at Finn and nodded.

"We need healers," Finn called. His mother stepped forward.

"We have fresh linens and water this way," she led the men, carrying the palettes with the wounded away. Tahra screamed when she saw Kai on one of the palettes and raced after him. Grabbing his hand in hers as the warriors followed the queen.

Odalis stepped out of a basket carrying a small bundle. Cairstine gasped beside me and raced to him.

"Your daughter, my lady," Odalis said.

"Thank you," she clutched the babe to her chest. "Thank

you so much. May I have your name so I may thank you properly?"

"I am Odalis, my lady," he bowed. "My mate is Cara, your nursemaid's sister."

"My thanks to you, Odalis," she said. "You have restored my child to me. Is Elspeth well?"

"Aye," he answered. "She and her son join us soon."

"Rhys? Rhys is coming here?" she asked.

My ears picked up on her quickening breath.

"So long as that is agreeable to you," Odalis watched her, clearly hearing the change in her breath.

"Oh, aye," she answered quickly. Looking down, she tried to hide a blush. "I thank you. They are dear friends."

Odalis bowed once more to her. "Then if you would forgive me, I wish to go to my wife and greet her."

"Of course, I thank you again," she clasped her daughter closer. Odalis left Cairstine and sought out Cara.

I stepped toward my friend, knowing how out of place she felt, when a gentle hand on my upper arm, stopped me. I looked over to see my husband. Finn's eyes searched mine, as mine did the same to him. He was hale and hearty. My husband had returned and for a moment I felt tears slide down my cheeks. Sybine's husband would never return to her. I threw my arms around his neck and kissed him as deeply as I dared. I was safe. He was alive and life grew within me.

I turned when I heard cheers and realized our clan was watching us. I blushed and melted into my husband's side. Then, catching Erina's gaze as she stood tall, I realized my position. I was going to be queen. I stood to my full height and smiled at our people.

"They missed you," Finn whispered in my ear, making me shudder.

"I missed them," I admitted. "I missed you."

"Dear god, I missed you too!" He kissed my neck and inhaled my scent. "Are you sure you are all right? And the bairn?"

"We are both fine," I assured him.

Someone called his name. He looked up and nodded. Looking back down at me, he kissed my nose.

"I love you," I said. "But our clan needs us."

"Our clan," he stated. "We are so lucky to have you. I, most of all."

"And I you," I kissed him once more.

"Be well, my love. Know that this evening, I will be holding you close and making you mine again. I love you and I intend to prove it," Finn said.

"And that will get me through the day," I said just before we broke apart to attend to our duties.

The story continues in *Will of Fire,* available soon!

 *cknowledgements*

Thank you so much for reading *Heart of Fire!* I hope you enjoyed Finn and Brigid as much as I did! This story went through a lot of edits and changes from the very first draft. But I am happy with how it panned out. Finn and Brigid are two of my favorites and from that first meeting with the wee knife to the last rescue, they continued to surprise me!

I am excited for the continuation *Will of Fire* and happy to say Cahal, Tahra, and Kai all have their stories told!

Until then, please follow me on social media with the handle; Author M. Katherine Clark for all my latest news!

And be sure to check out my Spotify playlist *Heart of Fire* for songs I listened to while writing!

Read on for a sneak peek of *Will of Fire*!

Will of Fire

M. KATHERINE CLARK

Chapter One

Sybine

Five years ago

Cahal was always so warm, but lying in the crook of his arm with the sun beating down on our skin, he was deliciously fiery. Though it was not our first time together, every time with him was like the first time. His rough fingers threaded through my hair as I snuggled deeper into the crook of his neck.

"I should be going," he said softly kissing my hair.

"Mmm," I moaned. "Donnae leave yet."

"I must," he replied. "Da' is making the announcement later today."

"What announcement?" I asked. He froze against met. Raising my head, I looked down at him, but he would not look at me. "Cahal? What's going on?"

"Nothing," he hurried to say.

"Cahal," I pressed. "Tell me."

"I am... asking to be the War Chief."

"War Chief?" I breathed. "War Chief is an unmatable position."

"Aye," he answered. "It is."

"And... me? Us?" I could not believe what he was telling me.

"You ken this is what I have always wanted. Are you wanting to hold me back?"

"I want to mate with you," I cried. He couldn't be doing this. Not today. Not after...

"And I want to mate with you, but War Chief is an honorable position and one I am eligible for. My position as second born does not give me any chance of leadership. This is my only chance."

"And what about my chance? I gave you everything," I cried. "I gave you my innocents! You swore you would mate me!"

"I never said that," he tried to justify. "Sybine, I do love you, but this may be my only chance."

So selfish. That's all he was. I should have known. I meant nothing to him. My virginity meant nothing to him. My future meant nothing to him. And the child I carried... meant nothing to him. Grabbing my dress, I pulled it over my head, sick to my stomach. Cahal did not try to stop me and I did not look back.

Bearcbhan

The tado my father had planned for today was going to be boring so I snuck out through the back and into the gardens where I could leave to the beach and shift. As I breathed in the fresh air of freedom, I stopped when I heard a sob. Looking around I did not see anyone but once I rounded the corner and looked through the archway of my mother's roses, I saw her. The Beautiful Sybine. My brother's future mate.

She was crying, hard. Glancing back, Cahal was nowhere to be seen. I could not allow her to cry any longer.

"Sybine," I called out. Immediately she sniffled and wiped her tears. I strode forward and sat beside her on the stone bench. "What is wrong? A woman as beautiful as you should never be crying."

"Please, go away Bearcbhan," she said. "I want to be alone."

"I will go," I answered. "So long as you swear to me you will stop crying." When she looked up at me, I was struck by her beautiful green eyes. She was so lovely. I read the sadness in her eyes. "What has happened?"

She sniffled, but soon a torrent of tears ran down her cheeks again. "Cahal," she gasped out. "Cahal has... he has petitioned to be War Chief."

What? That cannot be. Father would not allow it. That is an unmateable position and surely he would not leave Sybine... Oh gods, no.

"He does not want to mate," she cried. Immediately I placed my arms around her slim shoulders and held her to me. We were the same age but I could feel her grief as if it was my own. Damn him for treating such a lass the way he did. I know what she gave him and for him to toss her aside for a mere title was inexcusable.

"How could he do that to you?"

She sobbed against me and my arms tightened around her. "I am so sorry, lass. I ken it does nae help but I am so sorry."

"What am I going to do? I gave him everything. The clan will shun me. I will never be able to marry. I am damaged. He swore he would marry me else I would never have..."

"I ken," I tried to soothe. "But you are not damaged. We will no' shun you, we are your family."

"No one will ever want me. The cast off of the prince."

Her bitterness crushed me and I could not stop my next words. "I would."

She froze against me and I tried to bite back the words. Finally, she pulled slightly away and looked up into my eyes. She was searching for something, I did not ken what.

"Why?" she finally asked.

"Why, what, lass?" I asked.

"Why would you want me?"

I was not prepared for that question. How did I put it into words? I was not an eloquent male. I opened my mouth to speak but she stopped me.

"You know what it is I gave him." She flushed a deep red.

"Aye," I answered.

"And you still want me?"

"I donnae understand and never have; how it is accepted for a male to do as he wishes and no' a female. You are held to such rigorous standards. Nay lass, I care not that you gave your innocents away. It was yours to give, no one's to take." I leaned my forehead toward her but she pulled away and stood, her back to me.

"It is not only what I gave him," she paused and took a deep breath. "I believe I am carrying his child."

That took me off guard. I could handle the fact she was no' a virgin, most women I was with were not, but what surprised me was the horror she must be suffering. With child and alone. I stood, after a moment of silence and walked over to her, pulling her to me gently.

"I am so sorry for all the strain you are under. Let me help with that burden? I am under no delusion you love me. Nor am I naive enough to think you will not always love him. I do not want you to feel trapped but for your sake, and for the baby, I want to help you. I love you."

"You what?" She looked up at me with her innocent eyes surprised. "I love you. I believe I always have. I stayed quiet as you were my brother's but now he has done what he has done, I am at liberty to speak. I love you. And should you mate with me I swear to make you a good husband. I swear to take care of you. And make no designs on you until after the child is born. And this child," I covered her still flat stomach, "will be mine if you will have me. I would never force you, lass. I would hope one day you may grow to love me as well. If we were to mate, could you see yourself with me?"

I was trying to ask gently but dragons are very physical creatures and I could never consign myself nor a potential mate to no physical love. She took a deep breath before she raised her head and brushed her lips against mine. In that moment, my dragon roared and I held her to me giving her a taste of what she would have as a mate.

But I could not help and think I was getting the better end of the bargain. Her taste would have to sustain me a long nine months and beyond. As well as through my brother's challenge when we tell my father of our mating.

An angry Cahal was unpredictable and though he was not as strong as our eldest brother Finn, he was by far the best choice for War Chief. He could level entire villages with one gust of his powerful fire and a beat of his massive wings. To say I was scare of him, was an exaggeration but I was not looking forward to the battle and subsequent recovery, that is if he did not kill me.

Cahal

"We had many great candidates this time for War Chief and even though I am saddened that my dear friend decided to step down, I wish him health and happiness." Father stood on the raised dais in his best attire. Finn stood to his right and the old War Chief, my father's father's best friend sat to his left. The old male had been in the position for nearly sixty years and though the time had not been unkind, it was clear the man was ready to live out his days in peace.

My body still ached from the trials two days ago. Grueling was too kind a word. But it was nothing compared to the adrenaline coursing through me at the prospect I would be War Chief for my father and my brother, my best friend.

Finn grinned at me when I caught his eye. We were so very close in age we could almost have been twins but he was thirteen months older than me and closer than a brother. We fought well together and I knew when he took over for father we would work well with each other and lead the clan.

Sybine's reaction troubled me. She knew this would be the best opportunity for me but she was angry earlier. I could tell. I was hoping to speak to my father after the ceremony. Perhaps he could make an exception.

"The trials and games proved one dragon male among you is the best choice. As per tradition, he will have a day to think on his position and should he refuse the title, another among you will be chosen. Therefore, without further discussion. My son, Finn and I have agreed... Cahal, my son, join us up here as our new War Chief.

A sense of pride rushed through me as I heard my name and saw my father's smile. A grin spread across my face and my dragon preened in the back of my mind as the other males cheered. Taking the steps two at a time, I reached my father and brother who both greeted me with a warrior's shake.

"Congratulations, brother," Finn stated with his rakish grin. "I look forward to our partnership."

"As do I," I said. "But I must speak to you both."

Father turned and gave the nod for the musicians to begin. The noise drowned out our conversation.

"What is on your mind, lad?" Father asked.

"I am so very thankful and grateful for this opportunity but, I beg of you, I want to mate with Sybine. I want to serve you and Finn as War Chief it has been my greatest desire but... I cannot abandon Sybine. Not after what she gave me."

"You rogue," Finn chuckled.

"You ask me to strike down tradition for you to be able to marry the lass?" Da' asked.

"I love her," it was the first time I had said it out loud and for some reason it felt right. She was mine and I would fight for her.

"Dear me," father replied though I saw a twinkle in his eye. He turned to Finn. "What say you, son? He will be your chief."

"I say..." Finn paused and I nearly punched him to get him to hurry up. "So long as he does not become weak and fat like so many males when they mate, I agree."

"Weak and fat?" My father echoed. "Better not let your mother hear you say that."

"I swear I will not grow weak and fat and I will always fulfill my duties before any other." Could they not give me a clear answer?

"Then Father I have no issue with you... bending tradition," Finn said.

I turned to my father, my palms sweating. Father stared at me for a long time before his face split into a grin.

"It is granted, son. Go claim your mate and bring her back here so I may announce a mating in two days' time."

My heart soared. My beast roared inside my head. We would claim her before the others. We would have her. She would be ours.

"Da'!" Bearcbhan's voice came from the front. We all turned and even the musicians stopped playing. My world tilted on its head when I saw Sybine, my mate, clutching my brother's hand and hurrying behind him. All eyes followed them, I even felt Finn step up closer to me as if ready to defend my claim.

They stopped and bowed before my father.

"Bearcbhan, Sybine, what has happened?" Da' asked.

"The greatest thing, Father," he said clutching Sybine's hand. "This beautiful female has agreed to be my mate. We desire you to mate us as soon as possible."

"What?" I bellowed. I never raised my voice but in that moment my dragon shouted so loudly inside my head it was the only sound I could hear.

The crowd before me silenced as all eyes turned to me.

"What is going on?" My father asked calmly. My eyes never left Sybine but she did not raise her eyes to me. "Sybine? My dear?"

She finally looked up at my father, raised her chin and took a deep breath.

"It is my choice, my king," Sybine said. "Bearcbhan is the most honorable, loving, and caring male of my acquaintance. And since I am unspoken for and free to do as I will, I have chosen Bearcbhan as my mate. Please, I ask for your blessing."

"Sybine," my father sighed. I felt his eyes on me for a moment. Then he looked back at my traitorous mate. I could not speak. My ears rang. My world was crumbling. "Sybine," my father said softly. "Come here, lass."

I saw her clutch Bearcbhan's hand and I could not hold in my dragon.

"Leave her, you bastard!" my dragon shouted. Bearcbhan's eyes flashed to dragon slits but before he could say anything da' snapped.

"Cahal! I ken you are upset but I will nae have you disparaging your mother."

My body shook and though I could see all that was happening I could do nothing to stop it. My dragon roared and in a moment I was in my dragon form. Releasing my fire, I called for a challenge. I would challenge him, my brother, for my betrothed.

www.ingramcontent.com/pod-product-compliance
Lightning Source LLC
Chambersburg PA
CBHW070310040726
47501CB00018B/1371